MILES LEDOUX

THE IMPOSTOR

Winter in Veil, Book 11

I

erseus, can I ask you something?

Benno was sometimes irked by how few people in Veil, Vermont, understood ASL, but in this instance he was glad no one could hear his sister call him by his given name. "Benno," his surname, was by far his preferred moniker.

Of course, he signed back.

Are you sure you want to stay living in Veil?

Benno stared at Pam a full five seconds before shaking his head and laughing in spite of himself. "Only you," he said out loud. Then he signed, *You're just asking me this now?*

They were sitting in the bus station, Benno in his deputy's uniform, his petite sister bundled up so thoroughly she was hardly visible underneath all the layers. It was early February, and Veil's outdoor temperature was in the single digits. Pam would be leaving any minute.

It just seems like Veil has a lot of crime and violence for such a small town.

We caught the serial killer, Benno began.

It's more than just the serial killer. Last October, that SUV deliberately rammed you in your patrol car and injured you.

We caught those guys, too. Eventually.

And then you had that slew of kidnappings. I'm just starting to wonder if there's something wrong with this town. With this much violence, you'd think there was organized crime here.

During Pam's visit, Benno had carefully avoided mentioning Veil's mayor, Elijah Pressler, whom he and the rest of the sheriff's department knew was corrupt. He was just as careful now. *You've been here a whole week,* he signed. *Did any serious crimes happen?*

Pam gave an exasperated sigh.

I don't think this is really about Veil's crime rate, Benno told her shrewdly. *I think you're worried about something else.*

Hesitantly Pam signed, *I know you don't like to talk about it.*

Benno nodded slowly. *You mean Sheriff Dubowski.*

Yes. And that deputy.

"Yeah," Benno said out loud, heavily. Then, after a moment's hesitation, he signed, *I shouldn't tell you this, but the deputy wrote an apology to the woman she threatened.*

You mean the woman she tried to kill!

Benno rolled his eyes. "Fine, yes."

I know you have friends here, but wouldn't it be better for you to work in a sheriff's department where there aren't so many criminals?

Benno went still for a minute. His expression was neutral; anyone who didn't know him well would have no idea he was holding tight to his temper. *We're working really hard to get people to trust us again. When you say those things, it doesn't help.*

They will trust you again, Pam reassured him. *They'd be crazy not to. What I'm worried about is who* you *can trust.*

At first Benno stared at her uncomprehendingly. Then his jaw dropped in astonishment. *Wait, are you saying—*

I'm saying I want you to be careful.

I trust all the deputies! I trust Sheriff Grogan!

Like you trusted Dubowski and that other deputy?

That's not fair!

What has Grogan done to earn your trust that Dubowski didn't? How do you know she doesn't have secrets like he did? How do you know she won't hurt you?

"Oh, come on, Pam!" shouted Benno, making the other occupants of the waiting room jump. "Sorry—sorry, everyone," he quickly apologized. With a deep breath, he gathered himself. *With Dubowski it was hero worship,* he told her. *I wanted to prove myself to him. But Jen Grogan is one of the few real friends I've made here.*

If anything, Pam looked *more* worried by this.

She's a good person, Benno insisted. *Her whole family is. They've got integrity. You're right, this town can be dangerous. Yes, I've gotten hurt. But the Grogans were hurt worse than I was. It's been really rough for them. They need my help.*

With the air of one who is knowingly fighting a losing battle, Pam signed, *Perseus, your problem is that you can't tell the difference between someone who needs your help and someone who deserves it.*

Benno blinked. "What??" Had he misinterpreted something?

Pam's bus chose that moment to start loading passengers.

I'm sorry I upset you, she told him quickly. *I just want you to be safe.*

I'll be fine! Trust me.

Pam gave him a firm hug, then let go and signed, *You're the most trustworthy person in this town. Anyone who doesn't know that is an idiot.*

Mischievously Benno replied, *So you're saying I should be sheriff.*

That's not funny. She hugged him again.

Benno felt his anger dissipating. "I'll be just fine," he whispered as he held her. "You'll see."

3

* * *

In the weeks since Sheriff Dubowski's ignominious demise, his successor, Jen Grogan, had driven the deputies to exhaustion, but the results had been worth it. Grogan had clearly prepared for such an occurrence, despite it being unexpected. Her way of running the department was completely different from her predecessor, and the transition was difficult, especially now that the department was suddenly short two deputies— not to mention the troubling circumstances surrounding the changeover. However, Grogan's leadership had proven effective, and Benno was sure they were through the worst of it.

Benno arrived at the sheriff's station early for roll call. Grogan was already in her office, battling paperwork. She gave him a quick wave as he passed by. Benno hoped she still got some time to spend with her family, have a social life. Last month she'd admitted to him in confidence that she'd had a one-night stand, though she wouldn't say with whom.

In the break room he found Deputies Tan and Ziegler. One of them had brought doughnut holes. Ziegler held a handful while Tan held a cup of coffee. "I think it was a brilliant choice," the former commented. "He was always talking everyone's ears off because he had so much to say. Now he can say it in writing and leave us alone."

"I never minded listening to Chuck," said Tan, "and I like reading his articles. The trouble is, he keeps trying to put humor in them." She finished her coffee and left the room.

Benno helped himself to a doughnut hole. In a low voice he asked, "Have you asked her out yet?"

"No idea what you're talking about," Ziegler said crisply.

Deputies Trent and Powell soon joined them. Last to arrive was Deputy Derrick—a sure sign that things had changed.

When Keith Dubowski was sheriff, Derrick had always been the first to report for duty.

Something else had changed about Derrick: he had evidently decided to grow a beard. It might just have been Benno's imagination, but Derrick seemed to be growing it in the same style as Dubowski's, which was a little disconcerting.

A few minutes before roll call was scheduled to begin, Benno was pleasantly surprised to see a certain young woman walk in the door. It had only been four months since Violet first appeared in Veil, yet it was hard for anyone, he was sure, to imagine Veil without her. Violet was a short, attractive woman with amber-yellow eyes. Her long, dark hair had a purple streak on one side. She was in her early twenties, but her exact age was unknown, even to herself. Violet's life prior to October fifteenth of last year was a complete mystery.

Benno remembered meeting her that first day. When he'd heard there was a girl found with amnesia, he'd initially been skeptical, but as he spent time with Violet, he gradually came to believe she was the real thing. He'd helped her retrace her steps to a spot just outside of town. There, it seemed, Violet had received a head injury, but they never uncovered anything beyond that. Benno couldn't imagine what he'd do in her position—no identity, no past, no friends or family. She didn't even have the name, Violet, until Cy gave it to her.

Cyanne Grogan, the sheriff's sixteen-year-old daughter, was the first person Violet had met after waking up in Veil. When Benno first met Cy, she'd seemed standoffish, aloof, even haughty. Violet had brought about a change in her, and now Cy was friends with practically everyone.

Cy had never stopped trying to help Violet reclaim her lost identity. Although they were still far from reaching that goal, Cy had brought to light an important discovery: Violet possessed a capacity for perfect memory. Everything she saw and did, she could recall in full detail. This strange, miraculous power had enabled Violet to assist the sheriff's department in solving some local cases—including the mystery of the dreaded serial killer, whose reign of terror had claimed the lives of several Veil residents before Violet unmasked him.

The last few weeks, Violet had seldom been seen at the sheriff's station, as she was focused on helping her friends, the Dosley family, recover from multiple recent hardships. (Benno had volunteered to help, too, but given that those hardships had been caused principally by people in the sheriff's department, he could understand why the Dosleys had refused his offer.)

"Hi, Benno." Violet gave him a friendly wave. "Did your sister get off okay?"

"Couldn't get rid of her soon enough," Benno replied good-naturedly.

"Violet?" Sheriff Grogan leaned her head of her office. "What are you doing here?"

Violet entered the office and held out an object. "You forgot your phone charger."

"Oh." Nonplussed, Grogan accepted it.

"And also…I wanted to ask you something."

Grogan regarded her curiously. "Must be something important if it couldn't wait till I got home." Violet had been living with Grogan and her daughter in their house out in the country.

Violet took a deep breath. "I did an interview with Chuck Benz yesterday—about Joy reopening her store—and this morning he sent me a draft of his article for the *Chronicle*." After a moment's hesitation, she said, "He refers to me as Violet Grogan."

Sheriff Grogan didn't respond, but a twinkle shone in her eyes.

Benno decided this conversation was private and turned away—just in time to see the main entrance open yet again.

"I haven't said anything to him yet," Violet went on. "I wanted to ask you if... And, and also to ask Cy if, um..."

The new arrival was a man in his late forties with a mane of salt-and-pepper hair and a heavy five-o'clock shadow. Over his tall, trim figure he wore a fleece-lined parka, sweater, and worn corduroy pants.

"Violet," Grogan said with patient amusement, "of course you can use Grogan as your surname."

Benno thought the man looked vaguely familiar, but he was sure this wasn't a Veil resident.

"I still need to ask Cy," mumbled Violet. "She was still asleep when I left."

"I'm sure Cy'd be fine with it. And by that I mean she's been nagging at me to tell you to take our last name for ages now."

"Can I help you, sir?" Benno approached the stranger, who turned a pair of wary, pale gray eyes on him.

"Hello. I'd like to see the sheriff." The man spoke with what sounded to Benno like practiced politeness.

Benno turned. "Sheriff?"

Grogan was standing in her office doorway, enveloped in a hug from Violet. They were almost a foot apart in height, so the sheriff's chin rested gently on Violet's head. For a few moments Grogan didn't respond, then she softly patted the younger woman on the shoulder. Violet pulled away, and Grogan turned to Benno. "Yes, what is it?"

Benno turned back to the stranger. He was startled to see the man's expression, as if he'd seen a ghost.

"My god..." The man's jaw went slack and he stood there, staring.

Grogan came up to them. "Who is this?" she asked Benno.

"I don't know."

"Nicole!" The man passed a shaking hand over his mouth. "My god, it's really you! I thought I'd never see you again!"

He'd caught the attention of everyone in the station. Sheriff Grogan and six deputies turned as one to see whom he was speaking to...

And beheld a wide-eyed Violet Grogan staring back at him.

II

"Nicole, it's me! It's Wade!" The man wept with apparent joy.

Benno looked from him back to Violet, who seemed transfixed with shock.

All of the deputies' heads were swiveling back and forth between the two of them. Only Sheriff Grogan held her head still, her eyes on Violet. Her expression hinted at something deeper than shock.

"I—I'm your stepfather," the man went on. "Don't...don't you recognize me?"

Slowly, jerkily, Violet shook her head, her expression frozen.

"Just—look at my face. Just look." The man took a step closer. "I read about the amnesia, but I think if you just look... Just try and remember..." He took another step.

Benno heard a thud. Violet had tried to back away and had fallen over. The man let out a cry of concern and made to help her up. With a yelp, Violet scrambled backward. Deputy Tan was immediately at her side, helping her to her feet.

"No, Nicole, you don't have to be afraid! It's all right, just—"

"Sir!" Grogan interposed herself between the man and Violet. "I need you to step into my office. Right now."

The man's attention was still on Violet. If he'd tried to push past Grogan, the sheriff could of course have stopped him, but Benno stepped to her side, providing sufficient dissuasion.

Accepting things as they were, the man let himself be escorted to the nearby office. "It's all right," he told the pale-faced Violet. "I'm not going anywhere. We'll be together soon, I promise!"

Violet gulped audibly.

* * *

"Wade Browning, four-thirty-five Highway Twelve, Blossom, Connecticut." Benno copied down the information as Sheriff Grogan read aloud from Wade's driver's license.

"I, um, I'd show you Nicole's ID," stammered Browning, "but she had it with her when she disappeared."

Steely-eyed, Grogan handed him back his ID. "You arrived in Veil today?"

"Last night. By the bus. I'm staying at the B and B."

"Let me make sure I understand what's going on. You came to Veil because you thought Violet might be your stepdaughter, who disappeared?"

"She is! She *is* Nicole!"

"Why didn't you try to contact us first?"

"How would I contact you?!"

"By phone? Email?"

"I don't *have* a phone or email!"

Grogan and Benno exchanged glances.

"Look, I'm not a stalker! You can check, I don't have a criminal record!"

"Thank you, I will be checking on that," said Grogan. "Personally."

"I just want to take my stepdaughter home! She's been missing for four months!"

Grogan stood and took a few nonchalant steps. Benno recognized the signs of her entering "interrogation mode." Dubowski had also had one. His method had mainly involved sitting behind his desk. Grogan's brought her to her feet, pacing, passing in and out of the suspect's field of view.

"How long has...Nicole...been your stepdaughter?"

"Five years."

"Since you married her mother?"

"That's right. Andrea Frazier."

"Where is she?"

"She—died two years ago."

"So then Nicole's last name is Frazier?"

"Yes—no. She has her father's last name, Gunneson."

"When exactly did she disappear?"

"I told you, four months ago."

"What date?"

"Date—?!"

"Sir, if one of my daughters disappeared, I would know not only the date but the last hour and minute that I saw her."

"It was eight o'clock in the morning, but I don't know the date! I don't know dates or days of the week, except when I work security at the fancy hotel. I just remember saying goodbye to her. She was going to Maine to visit Moosehead Lake. She used to go there with her parents when she was a kid. Since her mother died, she—"

"She drove to Moosehead Lake?"

"No, she—she doesn't have a car. She was taking a bus."

"Was she living with you at the time?"

"Yes. Well, no, not exactly. My property has four cabins. She has her own."

"She's been living in your 'cabin' for five years?"

"Since she and Andrea moved in with me, yes."

Benno had to admire the man a little for holding up under Grogan's barrage of questions.

"They moved in with you five years ago in Blossom, Connecticut?"

"Look, what is this—?!"

"Mr. Browning, I happen to be familiar with Blossom. There are no schools anywhere nearby."

"Well, Nicole was home schooled!"

"Home schooled. Did you assist in her schooling?"

"Assist—?! No! She was all finished with school before she and Andrea moved in!"

"You said that was five years ago."

"She's twenty-three!"

This visibly threw the sheriff. She blinked several times. She, like everyone else in Veil, had thought Violet was younger, perhaps twenty or twenty-one. But the doctors had only said, *early twenties...*

"Look, why are you people giving me the third degree?! I assume you've been trying to help Nicole find her family so she can go home. Well, here I am!"

"How exactly did you find out she was in Veil?" asked Benno, giving Grogan time to recover herself.

"I used the computer at a public library. I saw an ad online, posted by the *Veil Chronicle*, back in October. It had Nicole's picture."

"Why did it take you so long to find that ad?" asked Grogan, crossing her arms.

"Well, I wasn't searching in Vermont! Not at first. I told you, she was on her way to *Maine*. I've no idea how she ended up here. When she didn't call me from Moosehead, I tried—"

"Call you? You said you don't have a phone!"

"My job! My job! She was supposed to call my job and leave a message for me! I tried to find out if she got off the bus at an earlier stop, but no one on the bus that day even remembered her! She'd just disappeared into thin air!" He rose to his feet, his voice rising along with him. "I've been going frantic for four months, and now I've finally found her, but you're treating me like I'm out to kidnap her!"

"Sit down, Mr. Browning," the sheriff ordered, unruffled by his outburst. When he obeyed, she went back to her chair and sat opposite him. "I apologize for the rigorous questioning. Since Violet came to Veil, I've assumed responsibility for her well-being. I...I've grown to care for her. I'm sure you can understand that."

Browning gave a nod, looking slightly mollified.

"So you can also understand that when a stranger appears out of the blue, claiming to be her family, I feel obligated to ask for proof before—"

"Proof? You want proof?" Browning pulled a manila envelope from his jacket pocket. With trembling hands he handed it to Grogan.

Benno sidled over as Grogan opened the envelope and drew out a wad of photographs. The first was of two people standing beside a wooden sign that read, *Summit: 2,454 feet.* Beyond them was a beautiful, lush mountain vista.

The two people were Wade Browning...and Violet, with his arm around her shoulders. They were smiling, flushed and happy.

One by one, Grogan examined other photos. They all showed more of the same: two people who were not only well-acquainted but on terms of deep affection.

Benno also noticed something significant: while her hair still bore the signature streak of purple, the scar from the mysterious wound that had likely caused Violet's amnesia was conspicuously absent from her forehead.

"Is that proof enough for you?" asked Browning.

* * *

Violet's expression was neutral as she went through the photos. Only the occasional twitch in her jaw revealed the stress she was under.

She was sitting in the corner of the break room, at the farthest possible distance from where Browning was sitting, watching her. It was almost noon.

Sheriff Grogan kept an eye on both of them from just outside the door. Three deputies approached her at the same time. "Talk to me," she said urgently in a low voice.

Deputy Derrick went first. "There's a plot of land near Blossom, Connecticut, that used to be owned by an Andrea Frazier. There was no official address; she had a post office box in town. The area's big enough that she could've been living off the grid in a cabin or shelter."

Grogan nodded. "Some people around here do the same."

"Five years ago, Frazier sold the land, and her mailing address changed to the one given by Browning."

"What about..."

"No record of a Nicole Gunneson at that address, but there is a birth certificate on file with the hospital in the nearest big town. She was born twenty-four years ago in September, to Andrea Frazier and Tom Gunneson. She has no driver's license. I also found a death certificate for Andrea from two years ago. Death by drowning."

Benno took up the report. "I spoke to the county police

department. There was nothing suspicious about Andrea's death. She was walking on a public trail by a river. She slipped, hit her head, and fell into the water, unconscious. They ruled it an accident."

"Did any of the officers see Nicole at the time?" asked Grogan.

"No, they only saw Browning."

"What about that hospital?"

"They have no medical records for any of them. And no missing persons report was filed for Nicole Gunneson, though the officer I spoke to said he vaguely remembered someone *trying* to file a report last October, and giving up because they got confused and worked up."

"Did he get any names?"

Benno shook his head.

"These people were seriously living off the grid," remarked Deputy Tan. "I combed through every social media platform and couldn't find profiles for any of them. It's kind of weird if you ask me—two hermits finding each other and falling in love? That sounds like a paradox or an oxymoron."

Grogan looked from one to the other, as if making up her mind about something. Finally she pointed at— "Derrick, get down to Blossom. Take as long as you need, but find me someone who knows Nicole Gunneson by sight."

"Yes, Sheriff," Derrick said resignedly. He headed toward the back door.

"I could call the police department back," Benno volunteered. "Make sure this is the real Wade Browning."

"Thanks, Benno," said Grogan, "but I've already checked up on that. This man is exactly who he says he is." Benno thought he heard dread in her voice. He would have put a hand on her shoulder if it had been appropriate.

Browning stood up, and everyone—Violet, Grogan, the two deputies—tensed. Browning took faltering steps toward Violet, who got jerkily to her feet. Her eyes never left him.

Browning stopped and spoke to her from three meters away. "I'm sorry if I came on too strong earlier. With your memory gone, I…" He made a show of holding back emotion. "I'm nothing to you. I get it. If you don't want me to be part of your life, I, um… I won't bother you again."

Benno saw emotion flicker in the sheriff's eyes.

"But if you ever want to know about your life before Veil, I can—"

"Who are you?"

Benno nearly jumped. He'd never heard Violet speak like that—gruff, accusing…dangerous.

"I told you, I'm Wade, your stepfa—"

"No. Who are *you*?"

Seemingly unsure of what she meant, Browning tried again. "I was born in Rhode Island. I inherited the land where I live. No family anymore. I have a sort of chicken farm. I sell eggs locally. Sometimes I work as a security guard at a fancy hotel. Was in the Navy for a little while. Honorably discharged after a head injury. My right eye's—"

"I'm not asking for a resumé," Violet snapped. "I'm asking *who you are*."

Browning gestured helplessly. "I'm…a hermit! At least, I have been since I lost you and your mother. I'm bad at conversation, so I talk mostly to plants and critters. I don't know all their names because I'm not much of a reader, but I know them all by sight." He glanced at Grogan, as if seeking help. "I don't know what else I can tell you. I didn't really—know myself until you and your mother came into my life."

When Violet spoke next, it sounded as if she were choosing her words very carefully. "How would you describe my memory?"

"Your memory?" Wade Browning looked completely at sea.

When Violet did nothing but continue her intense stare, Browning glanced again at the sheriff.

"She's trying to find out if you know something personal about her," said Grogan.

"Something personal… Oh! Yeah, of course I know about that!" He smiled brightly. "I was the first person you came out to!"

Benno made an involuntary movement.

Grogan drew a sharp breath.

Violet had a look of revulsion mixed with outrage. "How dare you?" she snarled.

"What? What did I say?" Browning looked flummoxed.

Grogan came to Violet's side and put a hand on her shoulder. Benno suspected it was as much to show support as to keep Violet from leaping onto the man.

"You want *that much*," Violet hissed, "to make me believe that I'm a loner at heart, that I would tell you something so personal—*you*, before anyone else?!" Browning tried to respond, but Violet plowed over him, "How convenient—if I'm a loner, I have to trust *your word alone!* No other witnesses! Not even a picture ID! Just documents! The only pictures of me are the ones *you have!*" She grabbed up the photographs and hurled them at him.

Deputy Benno spent the next minute helping the sheriff defuse the situation. At the end of the minute, Browning had been escorted from the room and was under supervision by Deputy Tan, leaving Benno, Grogan, and Violet.

Violet sat at the corner of a table and wiped her eyes. "Jen, he's a liar," she said pleadingly. "He's a fraud. Please say you believe me."

Jen sat at the end of the table and took Violet's hand. "Violet, you know I want to. But apart from that being selfish on my part, I also have an obligation to you as sheriff, so I have to tell you…he just might be telling the truth."

Violet shook her head stubbornly and sniffled. Grogan reached over and gently brushed hair out of Violet's face. Benno had seen her do the same to her daughter, Cyanne. Once again he felt he ought not to be within earshot.

"No matter what happens," said Grogan, "you don't have to stop being Violet. But as long as you are, you'll never be able to do the things normal people do—drive a car, have a paycheck with your name on it, fly on a plane, visit another country…"

Getting control of herself, Violet looked Grogan in the eye and said in an even voice, "I'm not Nicole."

Grogan thought for a minute. "Tell you what. Over the next few days, we'll keep trying to verify his story, but I suggest you spend some time with him each day, just in case anything he says resonates with you."

"I'm not going anywhere alone with him!"

"One of the deputies will always be there."

"Why not you?"

Grogan didn't answer, though Benno thought he could read the answer in her face: her heart was breaking already. She had no desire to help it along.

Grogan explained her plan to Browning and he readily agreed. Deputy Tan was a witness. By the end of the day, she and Benno had filled in the rest of the deputies on all that had happened, though Benno was discreet about the personal details.

III

On most days, Mayor Pressler ate lunch at his favorite restaurant near his office. Today, however, he announced to his secretary that he preferred to eat at home, and home he went. Home for Elijah Pressler was a mansion on the side of the hills overlooking Veil. Since he'd be leaving again in less than an hour, he parked his car in the curving driveway.

Just as he alighted, he stopped short.

The real reason for his coming home during the lunch hour was that he expected a certain delivery, which he desired to receive in person. Once out of his car, he could see that the package had already arrived and was lying on his porch.

There was something else on his porch which he had not expected to see: a very cross-looking Cyanne Grogan.

Pressler had known that this encounter was inevitable—in fact, he'd anticipated it happening much sooner than this—but now was certainly not the time he'd have chosen.

Cyanne marched down the porch steps and halted before him. The only greeting she offered was the hard glare she gave him.

Pressler did his best to keep his eyes on her and not glance too often at the package behind her. "I wasn't expecting any visitors today," he remarked mildly. When that elicited no reply, he went on, "I seem to recall another time you visited me without an invitation. On that occasion, I believe I made it clear to you that I'm not a good—"

"Wade Browning."

Pressler blinked at her several times. "Excuse me?"

"Wade—Browning," she repeated with sharp enunciation.

"I don't know who that is."

"I think you do."

"Well, I can't help you with that."

"So you're not behind it?"

"You haven't told me what 'it' is."

Cy gave him a piercing stare...then, apparently satisfied, she spat, "Okay, fine," and stepped past him.

Frowning, Pressler raised a finger. "Just a minute."

"No, I don't think so."

Growing irritated, Pressler snapped, "Cyanne—"

"NO!!" Cy whipped around and pointed straight at him. Her bark must have been heard by half of Veil.

In a lower voice she growled, "You do not get to lose your temper with me. Not today, not ever. You don't even get to be annoyed with me, not even if I..." She paused, apparently trying to come up with an example, but her anger seemed to overpower her coherency.

Pressler said quietly but firmly, "You came onto my property to ask me a question. Apparently you've gotten an answer. I'm entitled to know what—"

"Entitled?! *Entitled??!!* You have some nerve!!!"

"Cyanne—"

"You sent me an email pretending to be my *high school friend*—which is messed up enough on its own—and made me think—" She remembered, just in time, to lower her voice. "You made me believe my mom tried to have an abortion while she was pregnant with me." Tears formed in her eyes.

Pressler fumed. When he drew breath, it looked as if he were about to shout. "...Have you talked about it with your mother?" he said in a casual tone.

Cy's eyes nearly popped out, she was so dumbfounded. "You are unbelievable!!"

"Have you talked about it?"

Cy merely shook her head, her mouth wide open.

"I'm guessing you have. I'm also guessing she told you her story. Now you have a better understanding of your mother, something *I* didn't have until it was too late. The only reason it happened for you is because of that email message."

"No." Cy spoke with quiet rage. "We didn't work things out because of you. We worked things out *in spite* of you. And don't pretend you did it to get me and Mom to bond. You did it to get back at Violet. She did something you didn't like, so you tried to punish her by splitting up the only two people she thinks of as family."

Pressler shook his head slowly and firmly. "You would not have split up."

"You don't know that!"

"Yes, I do. I know people."

"Well, apparently you don't because I came this close to running away! I only had the chance to talk to Mom because I came back, and the only reason I came back was that I heard Violet was in the hospital!"

"What do you mean, you ran away?!" Pressler sounded genuinely thrown.

"I mean I was *on the bus!* I was literally leaving Veil! I packed up a bag and I—I left without even saying goodbye to my cat!

I'm a horrible person now, thanks a lot!"

A corner of Pressler's brain gave the logical response: that Cyanne hadn't said goodbye because she knew, deep down, that she wasn't really going to leave. But instead, Pressler stood there, flummoxed. "You…ran away…"

"Well, what did you expect me to do?!"

Pressler met her eyes and then looked away.

"Oh my god." Cy almost laughed. She shook her head slowly in disgusted wonder. "You thought I'd come to *you*. You would've played the wise hero. You would've poured me some tea, dried my tears, and promised it would be all right. Then you'd pretend to investigate. Oh, look—a miracle! What the email said isn't true after all! I could go home…because *you'd* made it a safe place again. And you would make sure Violet knew that the only reason she still had a family was because you were *allowing* her to have one. That's diabolical."

Pressler said nothing, though his face twitched with repressed fury and resentment.

"And since that plan didn't work, now you're trying to get Violet out of Veil altogether. You *are* behind Wade Browning, aren't you."

"Who is this Wade Browning??!"

But Cy was already marching away. She paused to say, over her shoulder, "You know, you're wrong. About what you said earlier. You can't just say I shouldn't expect you to do the right thing, like that's a naive thing to expect. That excuse might work on yourself, but it doesn't work on me. You're still capable of choosing right over wrong. Just like my dad, just like Rob, just like…" She blinked. "Wow, I have met so many awful people since I moved here."

"You can't lump me in with your father and your—"

"I'm not. You're better than they are. That's what makes you worse for doing what you did." With that, she strode off.

Pressler stood looking after her for a moment. He might have stood there a long time if not for his pressing need to get the package off his porch and into a safe hiding place, where it would wait until he had time to deal with it. He brought the package inside, shut the door behind him—and paused, once again distracted. "Wade Browning," he murmured to himself. Of course, Cyanne was right, Pressler knew who Browning was. He knew all about what had happened at the sheriff's station yesterday, though he could never admit *how* he knew, least of all to Cyanne. However, he had no idea where Browning had come from or what he really wanted.

And that rankled him.

* * *

Mayor Pressler was not the only one who was keen to learn more about the stranger in town. Deputy Benno had volunteered to accompany Deputy Derrick on his fact-finding mission to Blossom, but Sheriff Grogan couldn't manage with any fewer deputies in Veil. Benno had to content himself with making slight diversions from his patrol to drive past the bed and breakfast where Browning was staying. On one occasion, Benno managed to follow him home after Browning bought a sandwich, but the man never spoke to anyone, never pulled out a cellular phone or did anything else that might contradict his story. If he was an impostor, as Violet suspected, he was a very careful one.

Benno returned to the station to find Violet in the waiting area. Her outfit was colorless, even drab. Her hair was done up in a severe-looking bun. Never before had she appeared so. She saw Benno and gave him half a smile.

"First night out with alleged stepdad?" asked Benno.

Violet nodded stiffly. "Deputy Tan's escorting me. I'm just waiting for her."

"Where are you going for dinner?"

"Oriental Cookery."

Benno nodded approval. "Make sure to try the water chestnuts."

Violet didn't seem to be listening. She appeared to be following her own train of thought. Almost to herself, she said, "This isn't going to change anything. I'm never going to take his word for what he says I am. The only reason I'm doing this is so Jen will stop being so…"

"Selfless?"

Violet sighed in frustration. "She's afraid that I might throw away my chance to reclaim my identity and my freedom, just in case Browning is telling the truth. She thinks I'm afraid of leaving Veil because I've gotten used to it here. And I admit, she's not all wrong…but if I thought there was *any* chance that this 'Nicole' is me, I'd…"

"What makes you so sure you're not?"

"A feeling. Something—deeper than instinct."

Benno took a seat next to her on the bench. "For what it's worth," he said softly, "I think you're right to be skeptical."

Violet looked at him. "You do?"

"This woman, Nicole—if she exists—has spent her whole life living off the grid. She spends her nights out in the rough and wild. That doesn't sound like you."

Violet shrugged and said wryly, "It wasn't so bad when I went on that camping trip."

"You mean the one in November, with Trisha?"

"Um, yes." Violet cast a quick, furtive glance in his direction.

24

Trisha Sinclair was Benno's former fiancée.

"Well, I'm going to keep looking into Browning's background. Sooner or later I'll find something that doesn't add up. And we're still waiting to hear back about the photos he gave us."

In a strange tone of voice, Violet said, "They're genuine."

Benno blinked in surprise.

"Or at least they'll appear genuine. Stand up to any test. And you won't find any flaws in his story...apart from the fact that it's mostly unverifiable, all based on his word."

"What makes you say that?"

"Just a hunch."

Benno frowned at her. He had a hunch of his own that she was holding something back. In a speculative voice he asked, "Why would someone go to so much trouble to fake your past identity?"

Violet's shoulders came up to her ears in an exaggerated shrug. "I don't know!" she said in a falsely cheery voice.

It was not at all convincing. Violet had a thought that she wasn't voicing, and it was troubling her. No—it was more than that. Benno studied her closely, tried to decipher the look in her eye. He saw anxiety there, but there was something else. Regret? Not quite...

Guilt. Violet Grogan felt *guilty* about something.

Suddenly Benno understood. Violet thought she had a shrewd idea what Wade was after, and she *wanted* to tell someone—she felt that she *should*—but for some reason she was keeping silent, and it was eating at her.

Benno thought for a moment, then said, "You know, whatever happens, you'll always have a family here in Veil. No matter where you go or what name you go by, you can always come back. We'll be here for you."

Violet melted before his eyes. She looked away with an expression of anguish.

Benno waited quietly.

Finally Violet drew a deep breath. She was still looking away from him. "Benno...there's something I think I should tell you."

Benno shifted toward her. "I'm listening."

Violet turned to face him, and the anxiety in her eyes became more pronounced.

"You don't have to tell me if you don't want to," Benno assured her.

"No, I need to," she said. "I should've told you before." She swallowed. "Benno..."

Benno waited.

"I...I kissed Trisha."

"What??"

"On the camping trip. We kissed. It was just the one time."

"O-kay."

"And it was just kissing, nothing else."

"Got it."

"Are—you mad?"

Benno gave a dry laugh. "About my ex and my friend liking each other? No, I'm not mad."

"Good." Violet sounded relieved, but the guilt in her expression had deepened.

Benno chewed his tongue. "Listen—"

"Violet?" Deputy Tan appeared before them. "You ready?"

As Violet got up to leave, she hesitated, looked back at Benno, took his hand, and gave it a squeeze. "Thank you," she murmured.

As she and Deputy Tan left by the front entrance, Sheriff Grogan leaned out of her office. "Benno," she said, "I need you and Ziegler to go to the county coroner. We just got a call from the state police. Apparently there was a break-in."

"Why did the state police call us?" asked Benno.

"Because only one case file was tampered with: the file on Dubowski."

Benno and Ziegler immediately drove to the county coroner's office. There they found that while the documents pertaining to the incidents surrounding Dubowski's demise had not been touched, the evidence locker had been broken into. Some items were now missing: Dubowski's pistol, the shell casings from the five bullets fired, and the jacket Dubowski was wearing when he died.

"This doesn't make sense," Ziegler complained. "The case is closed. Why would someone steal the evidence? It's not like anyone was ever going to do anything with it."

"It could have something to do with the Dosleys," Benno said slowly, thoughtfully. "A few people in town still believe Joy murdered the sheriff, and they want her prosecuted."

"How does stealing evidence help build a case against her?"

"I'm not sure."

Another puzzling aspect of the break-in was that there was no sign of forced entry. In fact, the coroner had only discovered the break-in by chance: one of the employees had walked by, snagged her sleeve on the locker door and pulled it open, revealing that it was unlocked. Had it not been for her, it might have been months before the theft was discovered, if ever.

A search had already been made of the premises: the missing items were not in the building. No one from Veil had been there recently, as far as anyone knew. Surveillance footage showed no intruders, no abnormalities. It was as if the coroner had been robbed by a ghost.

Or a professional, thought Benno.

And if someone had hired a professional, that tended to implicate a particular person…

IV

If anyone were paying close attention, they might have wondered if perhaps Mayor Pressler no longer favored the bagel shop near his office, for twice in a week he chose a different restaurant at which to spend his lunch hour. His choice today was a small, Venetian-themed pizzeria on Main Street.

As he strode toward the restaurant's front door, Pressler rehearsed his cover story in his head, should anyone ask: this pizzeria was gaining fame as one of the best vegan cheese locations in New England, and he wanted to patronize businesses that would bring commerce to Veil.

A waiter met him just inside and showed him to a table, but halfway there, Pressler stopped and exclaimed, "Wait—Nurse Long?"

A thirty-one-year-old woman sitting in a booth looked up with wide eyes.

Pressler continued volubly, "Penny Long! Hi! It's good to see you again!" To the waiter he said, "This woman saved my life last December, when I fell through the ice." He turned back to the nurse. "I am so happy to see you! Mind if I join you?"

The woman's eyes were still wide, but anyone looking closely would've seen that they contained no surprise, only anxiety.

With an effort, she smiled and said, as brightly as she could, "Please join me."

She's no actress, thought Pressler with a mental eye-roll. He sat across from her in the booth and ordered coffee. When the waiter left, he made a show of looking at the menu.

Penny Long whispered, "Mister Mayor, you said you wouldn't—"

"Really!" Pressler set down the menu and radiated cheeriness. "That's wonderful!" Then, maintaining his expression, he continued in a lower voice, "Don't whisper, please. It attracts attention."

"But..." Penny was still whispering. "But people will hear—"

"And how are your children?" asked Pressler pleasantly.

"What?"

"You have four of them, right?"

"Y-" Penny cleared her throat. "Yes, I have four kids."

For several minutes, Pressler led her in improvised conversation. By the time Pressler's lunch arrived, Penny seemed—on the surface—much less anxious, and her speech much less conspicuous.

"Mister Mayor, can I say something?" she asked once the waiter had left their table.

"Much better," said Pressler. "A tense person always draws the interest of bystanders, but if they see you relaxed, they're less likely to pay any attention."

"Mr. Mayor, you said I wouldn't have to do this anymore."

Pressler nodded, though it was hard to tell if he was nodding in response to her or to the slice of pizza he'd just sampled. "At the time, I meant it," he said. "You did help save me, and I intended to reward that."

"Then why did you tell me to meet you here?"

30

"I wanted to ask you a couple things."

"What things?"

"Well, first of all...how is your house?"

Penny looked nonplussed. "My house?"

Pressler nodded and replied, with his mouth full, "The one you don't owe any payments on anymore."

Penny realized what he wanted her to say. "My house is fine... Thank you," she added in as normal a tone of voice as she could manage.

"And your youngest child, the one you adopted, shall we say, not quite legally—how is he?"

Penny swallowed. "Mr. Mayor," she said evenly, "I appreciate everything you did for me, I really do. But I never felt right, giving you confidential hospital information. I'm begging you, please don't make me do that again."

"That was very well said," Pressler complimented her. "Good eye contact. Very assertive. But as a matter of fact, what I want to ask you isn't confidential at all."

"O-oh."

"Not very." He smiled disarmingly.

"What is it?"

"A few weeks ago, you had Violet Grogan as a patient in the hospital. She had a head injury. Took her a day to wake up. What I want to know is...did anything happen?"

Penny blinked. "Did anything...happen?"

"Did anything happen," Pressler said slowly, "when Violet woke up in the hospital?"

"You mean with the deputy?"

"No, I don't mean the deputy," Pressler came close to snapping. "I'm just talking about Violet. I want to know if anything *happened* when she woke up."

Penny stared at him. "Mr. Mayor, I have no idea what you're talking about." When Pressler didn't respond, she went on desperately, "When Violet came to, we took her off the IV, gave her something to soothe her throat, and a few hours later, she went home. That was it."

"You didn't notice anything odd about the way she behaved?"

"No, nothing."

"She didn't say or do anything that caught your attention?"

"Well, like I said, her throat was too sore to say any—oh..."

Pressler leaned forward, his eyes bright. "What?"

"Well, she did actually say something—in her sleep."

This was clearly not what Pressler had been aiming for, but he remained interested. "What did she say?"

"She said one word several times over. At first I thought it was 'murder,' but now... Yeah, I'm pretty sure it was 'mirror.'"

Pressler raised an eyebrow. "Mirror?"

"Yes, sir."

"...Mirror..."

"Here's your credit card back, Mr. Mayor. Just need your John Hancock."

Heaving a disappointed sigh, Pressler took his credit card and signed the receipt. Once the waiter had gone away, Penny went back to whispering: "Mr. Mayor, can I please go now?"

Pressler regarded her tiredly. "Of course you can go. I'm not keeping you prisoner or holding you hostage. I'm not a villain!" That was perhaps what he wanted to say. Instead he gave a monosyllabic affirmative, and she made a hurried exit. Pressler couldn't even find the motivation to deliver an embellished goodbye: "So gracious of you to keep me company during my lunch hour! It was a pleasure speaking with you!" or some such garbage. No one was paying attention anyway.

No one except the waiter who had just been at their table, and had overheard part of the conversation. Deputy Benno returned the uniform to the manager and thanked him for the favor.

* * *

Benno meant to report what had happened to Sheriff Grogan right away, but when he returned to the station, she was out on a call. He'd have to wait until after he'd gotten back from escorting Violet on her last dinner with Wade Browning.

Violet had been out with Browning four times, always at the Oriental Cookery. She'd been escorted by Deputies Tan, Ziegler, Trent, and Powell. None of them had heard what Violet and Browning said to each other during their meal, but they all reported that Violet spent each evening sulkily resisting the stranger's attempts to engage her in conversation. Grogan had even mentioned that Violet had begun to be less chatty at home—and Violet had never been that talkative to begin with. Grogan said she and Cy were becoming concerned, and so was Benno.

However, when he met her in front of the sheriff's station, Violet seemed in higher spirits. "I can see the light at the end of the tunnel," she said when he inquired about her mood. "This is the last evening I have to spend with him. Deputy Derrick just got back from Blossom—he found zilch. No one's ever seen Nicole, if she even exists. So even if Nicole is me—which she's not—there's no way to prove it, so Jen will *have* to get off my back. I promised her I'd give him one last chance to convince me I'm his stepdaughter, but after that it's 'Goodbye, Wade!'"

She sounded buoyant, but Benno sensed something in her tone, a grain of insincerity. Again he felt there was something she yearned to tell him, that her heart wasn't fully in the act she was putting on. *She doesn't think Browning will leave once she's refused him,* Benno mused. *She's afraid he'll stay, but she hasn't told anyone the reason.*

Benno remembered how Violet had spoken about Browning a few days ago. *You won't find any flaws in his story,* she had said. She'd sounded quite certain.

She knows who Browning really is, he realized. *Or she thinks she does. Why hasn't she told us?!*

The question burned in his mind as he accompanied Violet to the restaurant. Wade Browning was waiting inside, at a booth across the room. He seemed chipper despite having failed four days in a row to convince Violet of their connection. Bracing herself, Violet headed over. Benno leveled at Browning what was meant to be a glare of warning, but Browning never even looked at him.

Sheriff Grogan had told Benno to give Violet and Browning plenty of space while still keeping them in sight, so Benno took a booth in the opposite corner. The restaurant staff had apparently grown used to the routine over the past week. It wasn't long before one of them brought Benno some crackers and a glass of water.

Benno knew Violet well enough to know she preferred to avoid confrontation when possible, but in his head he'd still imagined her challenging this man, testing him, setting traps and exposing him as a fraud. However, as he watched, Violet merely sat there while Browning talked on and on about who knew what. The only thing she showed interest in was her food, which, if Benno wasn't mistaken, was a dish of veggie lo mein with extra water chestnuts. Benno smiled to himself.

For over an hour, Benno sat and watched his friend, thinking about why she might be keeping secrets from those closest to her, wondering why she had been acting so strange lately, and considering why Mayor Pressler would suddenly be so interested in Violet's recent convalescence in the hospital. The ghost of a pattern began to form in his head.

At long last, Violet stood up and began bundling up for the cold. It hadn't snowed the last several days, but the temperature had dipped below zero more than once. Browning stood up as well, and finally Benno glimpsed dismay in his expression.

As Benno stood and made his way slowly over to them, Violet turned to Browning and said, "Well, thank you for the week's worth of Chinese food. Hope you have a safe drive back to Connecticut." Browning didn't answer. Violet and Benno headed for the exit. Benno felt Violet's arm twine around his.

From behind them came Browning's voice: "Nicole, I'm not giving up! Not ever."

Violet slowed, but only for a moment, and she didn't look back. She continued to hang onto Benno outside the restaurant. Benno's patrol car was parked down the street.

"Are you okay?" he asked her.

"I will be once I get home."

Violet's cell phone rang just then. She pulled it out and looked at the screen—and stopped dead. She looked up at Benno with a guarded, hesitant expression. "I—need to take this in private."

"Sure." Benno gestured to the patrol car.

"No, I don't want you to freeze. I'll just go down here." Before Benno could protest, she darted down a flight of stone steps leading to the basement of a clothing store. Several of the old buildings on Veil's Main Street had such steps in front. Benno would've insisted Violet accept the warmer option, but she was already speaking to whoever had called her, and he didn't want to intrude.

He started to slip into the patrol car, but a glance up the street arrested his movement. Someone was racing down the sidewalk toward him, somehow managing not to slip and fall. Benno squinted—yes, it was Wade Browning. Benno shut the car door and intercepted him.

"I just want to say one more thing to her!" panted Browning.

"No," said Benno, spreading his arms to block the man's way. "Your time is up. You can give the message to Sheriff Grogan, and she'll pass it on if she decides to."

"No, I have to tell it to *her!*"

"You can't talk to her without her consent."

Browning tried to dive past Benno, who caught him easily and put him in an arm lock. "This is your last warning! Walk away or I'm arresting you."

At that moment, Violet came back up the stairs to street-level. "No, I can't leave now!" she hissed in the phone. "It would be a dead giveaway that I—" She gasped when she saw the two men just a few meters away. Without another word, she ended the call and stuffed the phone in her pocket.

Before Browning could speak, Benno shoved him away and snarled, "Walk away! Do it! Say one more word, and I'll throw you in a cell!"

Browning hesitated, hovering indecisively.

"One word!" bellowed Benno.

Browning finally took the hint and trudged away.

When he was out of earshot, Violet came up to Benno and said apprehensively, "How much did you hear?"

This was not the question Benno had expected. He'd thought she'd been about to ask what Browning wanted. Benno frowned at her and said, "Nothing."

Violet nodded, apparently satisfied.

Once they were both in the car, she asked, "Could you do me a favor?"

"Name it."

"Could you not tell anyone about what just happened?"

Benno stared at her. "You mean anyone other than the sheriff and Cy?"

"Not them either. Especially not them. Please."

"Violet… Browning just broke the agreement. You might have been in danger just now. There's no way I'm not reporting this."

She looked at him steadily, her eyes pleading more than she could put into words.

The windshield misted as Benno blew out his breath. "I'll leave out the phone call if that's what you don't want them to know about."

Violet seemed to sense that was as far as he'd compromise. She faced forward with an odd expression. "Okay," she said distantly.

Benno started the engine and reached for the gear shift. He paused, turned off the engine again. "Violet, what's going on?"

She turned her head, gave him an anxious look.

"I know you're hiding something from us. I think you're doing it to protect us. I saw the look on your face when Browning first showed up. You had no idea who he was, and you still don't. But even though you don't know *who* he is, you know who he *is,* so to speak. And that's why you're afraid of him."

Violet turned away, but not before Benno saw tears in her eyes. She said thickly, "Please just take me home. I'm sorry."

Benno felt a pang of guilt. He re-started the engine and turned up the heat. He considered touching her supportively on the arm or the shoulder, but he decided against it.

Violet was silent all the way home.

* * *

"Mirror..."

Mayor Pressler sipped from a glass of whiskey as he stared at a decorative mirror over his fireplace. He knew he'd hit a dead end. The point of the alcohol had been to help him to stop thinking, stop trying to follow a clue that led nowhere, but he couldn't get it out of his head. "Mirror...mirror, mirror..." He paced about the room, muttering. "Mirror, mirror, on the wall, who in this land is the fairest of us all?"

He caught sight of himself in the mirror again. The corner of his mouth curled in wry amusement. Affecting a gruff, hoarse voice, he drew an answer from the mirror on his wall. "You, my queen, are fair, it is true. But Snow White is a thousand times fairer than you." His amusement faded. He resumed his pacing. "You, my queen... You, Mr. Mayor... Hmph. Instead of Snow White, I've got Violet Hair. Violet... Cyanne... Magenta... Azura—"

He came to a dead stop.

A dawning light shone in his eyes.

The glass of whiskey began to slip through his fingers. He could easily stop it from falling. All he had to do was turn away from his train of thought.

The glass shattered on the floor.

He darted back to the mirror. He peered into it hard, as if trying to see something in it besides himself. When his breath fogged up the glass, he scrubbed it away impatiently with his sleeve.

His reflection leaned in close and hissed, "Is it possible??"

Pressler didn't have an answer... Yet.

V

When his alarm clock went off, Benno wondered why the sky hadn't yet turned pink with false dawn. Perhaps it was a cloudy morning. Was Veil in for a surprise snowstorm?

Then he realized it wasn't his alarm clock. His phone was ringing. The screen told him it was Sheriff Grogan calling.

He answered the call. "Go, Sheriff," he managed to say with a minimum of grogginess.

"Benno, I need you here right away."

"What's happened?"

"Someone's tried to murder Wade Browning."

* * *

Benno met Sheriff Grogan at the bed and breakfast where Browning was staying. Other deputies were already there, processing the room as a crime scene, though it looked relatively undisturbed.

"Browning called the station an hour ago," Grogan told him. "Deputy Derrick took the call. Browning was having trouble breathing. He begged for help and then collapsed."

"Will he make it?"

"The hospital thinks so. They also think he was poisoned, but they haven't found any foreign substance in his body."

"Not even something he might be allergic to?"

"This wasn't an allergic reaction."

Benno joined the other deputies in the search for evidence that someone other than Browning had been in the room, or had put something in it that had poisoned him. An hour and a half later, when they all trudged off in search of breakfast, they'd turned up nothing.

No sign that Browning was attacked, thought Benno, *just like there were no flaws in his story and his background. Both appear innocent—and they're both obviously suspect. It can't be a coincidence.*

Grogan had her cell phone to her ear. "Cy? I know, I'm sorry to wake you. Get Violet and put her on the phone, please... What? What do you mean, she's gone?! Where is she?!!"

* * *

"I was down at Riverbend Park," Violet said with a shrug.

Sheriff Grogan stared at her across the station bullpen. The last several minutes had been a frantic prelude to a full-scale search, full of barked orders and spontaneous mobilization, all brought to a screeching halt when Violet walked nonchalantly through the front entrance.

Grogan looked torn between hugging her and taking her head off.

Seeming to realize a grave situation was afoot, Violet asked, "What's going on?"

Before anyone could answer, Grogan pointed and snapped, "Office!" She stormed across the room and then, just before following Violet out, she turned back and ordered, "Cancel the—the...everything!" With that, she steered Violet into her office and closed the door.

The sheriff's office was across the hall from the bullpen,

where a row of workstations, each equipped with a phone and a desktop computer, allowed the deputies to coordinate searches and other crisis management. Between calling back the radio station and telling them *not* to interrupt the morning's broadcast with a special report, and other such communications, the deputies cast glances through the picture windows that gave a view of the hallway. Through the glass in the sheriff's office door, they saw Violet standing before the sheriff's desk. Grogan, standing (presumably) behind the desk, was out of view, but Violet was plainly listening to her speak. Whatever Grogan was saying must have been shocking, for Violet's mouth dropped open in horror. At first she said very little, but then, after listening some more, she shook her head and spoke a word that was clearly "No." She said it a few more times, between what must have been Grogan's questions.

"What's going on in there?" asked Ziegler.

Violet continued to shake her head as she spoke, adding a helpless shrug.

"Sheriff just asked her if she has any witnesses at Riverbend Park," Tan clarified grimly.

"There's no way she thinks Violet could've attacked Browning!" huffed Ziegler.

"It's still her job to ask," Benno pointed out.

This statement seemed borne out by the fact that tears were now rolling down Violet's cheeks, though she bravely kept control of herself and continued answering questions.

Benno watched, feeling sorry for both the women in that room.

Violet was losing control now, her jaw trembling, her chest heaving with sobs. The view through the door was suddenly blocked by a flurry of motion. Next moment, Grogan's arms were wrapped tightly around Violet, who buried her head in the woman's chest, shaking. They turned such that Grogan's face was visible. Her eyes were closed, but her troubled expression stood out. Her mouth moved, speaking what might've been "I'm sorry," and "It's gonna be okay."

By the time Grogan opened her eyes, every deputy's head had turned tactfully away.

A few minutes later, the sheriff re-entered the bullpen and said, in as official a voice as she could manage, "I'm leaving briefly to take Violet home. Continue the investigation. Derrick will stay on guard over Browning at the hospital." She threw a furtive glance behind her. Violet was still in Grogan's office, blowing her nose. In a lower voice, the sheriff said, "Tan, call the hockey pavilion, ask them to send over the footage from their outdoor security cameras from this morning, that is assuming they keep their—" When Violet entered, Grogan's voice went back to normal. "I'll be back shortly. Keep me posted with developments."

"Has anyone checked on Megan Toombs?"

There was no comprehension in any of the looks directed at Violet. Sheriff Grogan blinked twice and gave her head a little shake. "What?"

"I was just wondering," Violet said in a halting voice, "whether anyone has seen Megan lately. I haven't seen her for some time and I just wanted to make sure she's okay."

Deputies Tan and Ziegler exchanged quizzical glances.

The sheriff looked totally at a loss. "Why would…?"

Violet's lips parted, but she made no reply. Only her eyes betrayed that she was struggling for a plausible answer that didn't exist.

"I'll check on her," Benno volunteered.

42

V

Grogan and the deputies turned to him in surprise.

"I'll drive over to her house and come right back."

Though bemused, Grogan seemed disinclined to argue. "Fine," she said.

Violet shot Benno a look of gratitude just before she left.

* * *

As Benno climbed the three sets of stone steps to the porch of the Toombs house, he couldn't help glancing up the road at one of the neighboring houses. The investigation of the break-in at the county coroner's office five days ago had gone nowhere, and although Benno still had a hunch Mayor Pressler was involved, there was no evidence to justify getting a search warrant for his home, or any of his other properties around town. *If he had the missing items—for whatever reason—he's probably gotten rid of them by now,* Benno thought.

When he was alive, Sheriff Dubowski had launched a number of investigations into Pressler's business affairs. Though nothing had ever been proven, Pressler was suspected of involvement in all kinds of criminal activities in other parts of the country—smuggling, fraud, counterfeiting—and Dubowski was determined to prevent him from bringing that criminal element here to Veil. In the days leading up to his death, the previous sheriff had even gone so far as to prepare for the possibility of Pressler having him killed. However, in his final hours, Dubowski seemed to undergo an inexplicable one-eighty, recanting his ongoing suspicion of Veil's mayor. Dubowski, of course, could never now explain this contradictory behavior, though Benno was determined to learn the answer someday.

Since becoming sheriff, Jen Grogan had done nothing to probe into Pressler's affairs, as if she trusted in Dubowski's last-minute reversal—but Benno was sure that wasn't the case.

When he'd told her about the conversation he'd overheard in the pizza joint, proving a long-held suspicion that Pressler had spies throughout Veil, controlled via extortion, Jen had ordered Benno not to go after Pressler but had applauded his initiative. "You did the right thing," she had said, "just at the wrong time." She wouldn't elaborate any further. Benno had a hunch she was forming a strategy to deal with the corrupt mayor; it just wasn't yet ready for implementation. He tried his best to curb his impatience. The sheriff knew he'd be there for her when she needed him.

Benno stumbled. Having been built on the side of a mountain along with the other high-income homes in Veil, it made sense that the gigantic house had so many steps, but it still felt obnoxious. After pausing a moment to catch his breath, Benno rang the doorbell.

The door was opened by an attractive woman in her late forties. Her hand made an absent, automatic brush at her hair, which looked like she'd just had it done. Benno had never met Megan Toombs's mother personally, but he had no trouble recognizing her, given her history with the sheriff's department. She regarded him with polite wariness. "Can I help you, Deputy...?"

"Benno, ma'am. I—"

"Are you a new deputy?"

"No, ma'am, I've been with the department a little over a year."

Mrs. Toombs's eyes narrowed a little.

Benno hurried on, "I just stopped by as a favor to Violet."

Mrs. Toombs instantly became friendlier. "How is Violet?"

"Well, that's a little up in the air at the moment."

"Oh, I heard about that man claiming to be her stepfather—obviously he's an impostor. And I don't believe someone tried to kill him in his hotel room. He was just about to leave Veil, wasn't he? I think it's obvious he poisoned himself, or he faked it. Wait, the sheriff doesn't suspect Violet, does she?"

"I don't think so."

"You don't *think* so? Does Violet need a lawyer? Is that why you're here?"

"No, ma'am. Violet just asked me to stop by and check how Megan is doing."

"Megan?" Mrs. Toombs was taken completely by surprise. "Why is she wondering about Megan?"

To this, Benno had no answer, for in truth he had no idea. He'd been half-hoping Mrs. Toombs could shed some light on the question, herself, but it was clear she was just as much in the dark as everyone else.

"Megan's not involved in this, is she? Is there something I should know?!"

"No," Benno assured her, thinking quickly. "It's just that Violet had been planning on looking in on Megan anyway, but Sheriff Grogan is restricting her movements and contacts for her own safety. In a sense, she's grounded."

"Ohh." Mrs. Toombs nodded in vehement sympathy. "Well, you can tell Violet that Megan is doing just fine. In fact, just last month she was recognized as a math prodigy. You know, so many kids—girls especially—are convinced at an early age that they aren't smart enough to understand math and science, like it's something only *really* smart kids understand. But I think it's really this convincing that's holding them back. Don't you think so?"

Benno thought there was some truth in that, but he could smell a one-sided conversation coming, so he kept his answer to a simple "Yes" in order to avoid it.

It didn't work. "The same thing almost happened to Megan. She had this horrible fifth-grade teacher. Last year she was failing his math class, which should tell you something about his teaching because she was doing fine everywhere else. It was only *his* class giving her trouble, and it had her thinking she was just bad at math. But then she had this wonderful *sixth*-grade teacher…"

Once Benno was able to escape, he called the Grogan house. Cy answered the phone.

"Violet's not up to talking right now," she said, *"but I'll tell her you went and made sure Megan's okay."* She cleared her throat.

A bell went off in Benno's brain. He'd known Cy long enough to recognize when she was lying or hiding something. Clearing her throat was her tell.

He said, "Thanks. And try not to worry. We're gonna find out what happened to Wade Browning."

"Good," said Cy, and then, apparently as an afterthought, she added, *"Yeah."*

She knows, thought Benno. *Violet told her who attacked Browning. Whether she was behind it or not, Violet knows the truth, and she's* still *not sharing it with us.*

As soon as Benno got back to the station, he spoke to Sheriff Grogan in private and reported his suspicions.

The sheriff nodded very slowly. "I've had a feeling Violet's been holding something back," she said slowly, "but I had no idea about Cy. I can usually tell when she's keeping something from me. Or I thought I could."

"I think Violet is afraid she'll endanger us if she lets us in on what she knows," said Benno.

"Well, she should let me be the judge of that. Anyway, if Cy knows something, I'll soon get it out of her."

There was a knock at the door. Deputy Ziegler stuck his head in. "Sheriff, we've got the footage from the hockey pavilion."

The footage showed Violet walking through the parking lot toward Riverbend Park half an hour before Browning called for help. She walked past the security camera in the other direction twenty minutes before she showed up at the station. It was evidence in her favor, but Violet still could have left the park between the two sightings—evading the cameras—gone to the bed and breakfast, and had enough time to attack Browning before returning to the park to fabricate her alibi.

Benno figured to himself that if Violet had faked an alibi she could've concocted something much more airtight, but at this point the only thing keeping her from being suspect number one was the fact that they still had no idea what had actually happened to Browning.

Sheriff Grogan ordered the deputies to go over Browning's room again, and to badger the hospital until they provided information that was helpful.

By the end of the day, they'd still turned up nothing.

* * *

Again Benno woke to his phone blaring. It was a much earlier hour this time. It was pitch black outside.

All Benno could manage when he answered the phone was, "H'llo?"

"Benno…"

It was the sheriff's voice, but there was something in it that hadn't been there before. Her job required a sense of urgency, but what Benno heard was deeper than that. Jen Grogan was calling not as the sheriff but as a mother.

As this permeated Benno's sleepiness and reached his brain, he pushed himself up to a sitting position and said, "I'm here."

"Violet's gone. And so's my car. The smoke detector started beeping 'cause it's low on batteries, and when I got up to change it, I... I never would've known otherwise."

"Wait, wait—Violet can drive?"

"She's in her twenties, Benno. And she has a perfect memory, so even if she hasn't driven since coming to Veil, she could learn just by watching!"

"Okay, I'm sorry."

"No, no, I'm sorry. I just—I couldn't get anything out of her or Cy earlier. My gut tells me there's danger. I feel like I have no control. Do you have any idea where she might've gone?"

Benno did, in fact, have a hunch. He volunteered to go check, himself.

During the reign of terror by Veil's serial killer the previous year, there was one victim that went largely unmentioned alongside the others: Benno's car. *Better your car than you!* his sister had told him, and he knew she was right, but Benno still allowed himself the occasional self-pitying grumble. These days he drove a pickup truck lent to him by Hal Clayton, the Veil sheriff's department's former senior deputy. Hal had been helping out Sheriff Grogan in an unofficial capacity since Dubowski's demise, which was a surprise for some. Many remembered what close friends Hal Clayton and Keith Dubowski had once been, and expected Hal to be up in arms with the department for letting Dubowski's name be dragged through the mud. Nevertheless, Hal had been nothing but generous with his assistance, and had made no public comment about Dubowski other than that he had confidence in the department's ability to interpret evidence.

Benno drove the pickup truck up the side of the mountain, into the neighborhood where Veil's wealthier citizens resided.

On an incline, the roads wound and forked rather than criss-crossed, and Benno made sure to park the truck before reaching the curve that would bring him within view of the Toombs house. Sure enough, when he got out and walked around the curve, he spotted the Grogan sedan parked just ahead of him.

Violet didn't seem too startled when Benno tapped on the window. She almost looked as if she were expecting him, in a weary sort of way. When she unlocked the passenger door and let him into the car, he was struck by just how exhausted she appeared.

"You know," he said casually, "for a stakeout, you should really be parked closer to the place you're watching."

Violet turned tired eyes toward the Toombs house. "No," she said. Fatigue slowed her voice to a hoarse crawl. "I think this is close enough."

Benno heaved a deep sigh. "So...how long?"

"I honestly don't know. I waited until I was sure Jen and Cy were asleep, and then I—"

"No," said Benno. "I mean...how long has it been since you got your memories back?"

VI

"Well, this is anti-climactic," sighed Violet. She didn't seem at all dismayed at Benno's deduction. If anything, she sounded relieved.

Benno found himself staring at her in fascination. For almost four months, Violet had waited for her memory to be restored, to re-discover who she was. Surely he wasn't alone in having pictured what it would look like—tears of joy, cries of wonder, a contagious jubilation filled with recovered life stories. Contrary to his expectations, the woman beside him was clearly burdened by what she'd found, not set free.

"What gave it away?" Violet asked, sounding semi-interested.

"There were lots of little things," Benno began. Then it occurred to him that what had mainly given him a hint was the conversation he'd overheard between Mayor Pressler and his spy from the hospital. Pressler had suspected before anyone else that Violet had her memories back, and guessed it had happened as a result of her head injury. He'd been fishing for confirmation from the hospital nurse.

Benno needed time to process this new development before tackling that complication, so he answered, "Mostly it was how sure you were that Browning was a liar and an impostor. Anyone who really couldn't remember her past would have at least a *little* bit of doubt, but you had no doubt at all. And then there was the phone call yesterday. The way you were talking to the person so secretively, it could only be someone you're close to. But lately you've been closed off from Cy and the sheriff."

The more she listened, the guiltier Violet looked.

"The person on the phone—it was someone from your past, wasn't it? The 'dead giveaway' you mentioned was your memories returning."

"I've wanted to tell everyone the truth. So badly."

"I think Cy's already figured it out on her own."

"Oh God." Violet buried her face in her hands.

"Violet," Benno said gravely, "you don't have to tell me anything if you're not ready to, and I know you think you're protecting everyone by keeping secrets...but—"

"My real name is Stephanie." She went still for a moment, then she clapped a hand over her mouth to stifle her sobs. She, herself, seemed stunned by her reaction. "I'm sorry," she tried to say, shivering horribly.

Benno reached over and started the engine—and the heater. He waited silently till she'd regained control of herself.

"I...I mean, my name *used* to be Stephanie. Stephanie Newcombe. I'm... I mean, I was... I'm—"

"What happened to Stephanie?" asked Benno.

Violet flashed him a look of gratitude. "She, um... She had a pretty rough life. Never knew her father. Mother was arrested when she was a baby, died in prison. Stephanie was raised by her older sister." She gave a sigh, perhaps of remembrance.

Benno grunted. "So was I."

Violet looked at him. "I didn't know that." She looked as though she'd rather hear about his past than disclose more about hers.

Gently, Benno kept her on track. "When did Stephanie discover her memory was better than everyone else's?"

"Only a few years ago. Her sister became an alcoholic and lost custody of her. Stephanie went in and out of foster homes, changed schools a bunch of times. She did okay in her classes, but she never graduated." A nauseated look came over her, and she went on quietly, "She ended up living in Rhode Island with an older man who said...who promised to take care of her."

In a measured tone, Benno asked, "Did he?"

"At first. Then Stephanie discovered she wasn't attracted to...people with penises. She thought it would be safe to tell him." For a moment, her mouth tightened in anger. "I wish all law enforcement agencies were like yours. Some of them, if you tell them a man tried to beat you and rape you, but there's not a scratch on you, and the man's a bloody mess because of a lucky..."

"They didn't believe you."

Violet gave a humorless laugh. "You wanted to know what I was hiding." She looked straight at him. "I'm a fugitive. Wanted for..."

"Defending yourself."

"I can't ask you to cover up for me—"

"And you've been on the run since then?"

"Pretty much," sighed Violet, "though technically there wasn't that much running involved. One of the foster families I was with had a cabin they barely used anymore. And having a perfect memory means that I can look at a map once and be able to walk for miles to a destination without ever going near a road or highway—as long as it's daylight. I also had some help from a girl I was, um..." She trailed off.

"And this was still in Rhode Island?"

"Vermont, actually." She laughed softly to herself. "It's trickier during certain months of the year, but if you know what you're doing and you don't mind being lonely all the time, you can always find an empty lakeside cabin to crash in."

"There are some lakeside cabins just a few miles from here," Benno remarked.

"Yes, there are," Violet said with significance. "Only those cabins are barely ever used. I thought at the time that that was a good thing, but not only are they seldom lived in, they're seldom maintained." Her fingers brushed the scar on her forehead. "Middle of the night, last October, there was an explosion. A propane tank, I think. I was lucky I was outside when the cabin blew up, but I was still close enough that I got hit by shrapnel."

Benno's mouth dropped open in shock.

"I must have wandered for hours in the dark, delirious, until I collapsed."

"On the highway just outside Veil?"

"Mm-hm." She inhaled deeply. "And now you know my story. The only one who knows it."

Benno reflected for a moment. It was true, after months of mystery and wonder, the story behind her appearance in Veil was anti-climactic, as she'd said. But it was also something else.

"At night?"

"Pardon?"

"You were outside at *night* when the cabin blew up? What were you doing outside?"

After a pause, Violet said, "Fishing, believe it or not. When you're trying to avoid human contact—"

"It wasn't because you were hiding from someone?"

"No!" Violet swallowed, then went on more calmly, "No, I—I haven't seen the man who assaulted me in over two years."

You've got to be kidding me, thought Benno. Aloud he said, "And this Wade Browning, you think he's a private detective hired by that man?"

Violet nodded.

"Then who tried to kill him?"

She looked straight at him. "I have no idea."

At least that's true, Benno decided. "And why haven't you told all of this to Cy and Jen?"

"The moment I tell them I'm a fugitive, they become accessories, just like you are now. Jen could get in serious trouble for aiding and abetting."

Benno laughed in spite of himself, drawing a look of surprise from Violet. "I'm going back to bed," he said.

"What?"

"I can't help you until you tell me the whole story. I don't know what it is, but you're still holding something back."

"I'm not!"

"Why are you playing guardian angel to Megan Toombs?"

Violet's eyes dropped.

"You said I'm the first person to know your story. Well, I'm not, because you haven't finished telling it yet. So I won't tell anyone else until you decide to come out with it."

Violet seemed quite touched by this. She closed her eyes and said, "You're a really good friend, Benno."

Benno hesitated, then decided on tough love. "Well, maybe you should start treating me like one. Goodnight."

He got out of the car and didn't look back.

When he got home, he fell into bed but couldn't make himself go back to sleep. After fifteen minutes, he got up and went to his computer. A brief search brought him information on Stephanie Newcombe, age twenty-two, wanted for aggravated assault against John Falk, a fifty-three-year-old insurance agent. There was no photo of Stephanie. The crime had been reported almost three years ago. Falk had apparently been blinded in one eye by the incident. Other women had, in the past, filed charges of assault and harassment against him, but none of the charges had ever stuck. The women were all under twenty-five.

Another search yielded reports on an exploded cabin near Digley Flow, Vermont. It had happened on October thirteenth of last year. The cabin was eight miles from Veil. Results of the investigation were inconclusive, so no one was sure how or why the explosion had occurred.

When Benno finally dropped off to sleep, he had a dream that shadowy figures were chasing him around a cabin beside a lake at night. One of them shot at him with a silenced gun, missed, and hit a propane tank. The world erupted in flame.

Then he dreamt it was four months later, and one of the men who had been hunting him showed another one his phone screen and said, "We didn't get him. He's still alive." On the screen was an image of Benno with a scar on his forehead, a streak of purple in his hair, and a caption below the photo: *Do you know this man? Amnesiac appears in Veil, VT...*

* * *

The sky had just started to lighten when Violet made it home. The moment she walked through the back door into the kitchen, Cy caught her in a tight embrace. Violet clung to her and took several deep breaths. It had been a long night, one of the longest she could remember.

Jen came into the kitchen and gave a sharp exhalation of relief. "Violet..."

Abruptly, Violet let go of Cy and beat a hasty retreat up the stairs. Jen was left sharing a look of concern with her daughter.

* * *

Deputy Benno half-expected his colleagues to tease him the next morning about his haggard appearance, but when he arrived at the station, no one seemed to notice. In fact, they all looked just as fatigued as he was. Perhaps last night had been sleepless for everyone.

Apparently the only person adept at hiding her exhaustion was Sheriff Grogan. When she called Benno into her office, he could barely make out any circles under her eyes.

"Violet's fine," she said when he asked her. "I don't know what you said to her last night, but she finally opened up to me and Cy this morning."

"How much did she tell you?"

"Not everything, I know, but I'm pretty sure she filled me in on everything she told *you*. She still hasn't explained what any of this has to do with Megan Toombs, but I think, given time, she'll tell us the rest."

"Should we fill in everyone else?"

Grogan pursed her lips, thinking. "Not yet. If it had any bearing on the attack on Browning, then yes, but as far as I can see, it's unrelated."

"Are you sure?" asked Benno.

Grogan looked at him sharply. "Do you think there's a connection?"

"I—don't know." When the sheriff didn't reply, he went on, "It's a feeling. A gut feeling. I've nothing to base it on. But it's there."

With a frown, Grogan said, "If Browning was hired by Violet's...former attachment, and if the attempt on his life is connected, then the only person who could've attacked him is Violet. Do you really think she'd do that?"

Quietly Benno answered, "Are we sure about who really hired Browning?"

"Well, who else could it have been?"

It was time for roll call, so the meeting ended on this nebulous note. Grogan and Benno went into the hall, where four other tired deputies joined them. As one, they plodded toward the bullpen.

"Where's Derrick?" asked Ziegler blearily.

"At the hospital," said Sheriff Grogan as her phone dinged. "On watch over Wade Browning." She pulled out her phone and frowned at the screen. "What on...?"

"What's wrong?" asked Benno.

"It's a text from Violet. She just got a call from Mayor Pressler. He told her he has information about the attack on Wade Browning. He wants her to meet him at his office right away—alone."

"No way," Benno said immediately.

"Why would he tell *Violet?*" wondered Ziegler. "Pressler's as friendly with her as he is with us, isn't he?"

"It almost sounds like he's trying to *blackmail* her," said Deputy Tan. "Like he thinks *she's* the one who attacked Browning, and he wants her alone with him so he can threaten her."

Grogan had been typing and sending a response, and now her phone dinged again. She groaned. "I ordered her not to go see him, but she's going anyway. Cy's a bad influence on her."

"I'll go with her as backup," Benno volunteered.

There were other volunteers, but the sheriff held up a hand and said, *"I'll* go. In the meantime, Tan, you're in charge."

In her wake, Grogan left behind an air of bemusement. She had not yet chosen a senior deputy, and when situations had called for it, she'd treated Derrick, the deputy with the most experience, as her second-in-command. Now, however, it seemed someone else might possibly receive the promotion, and Tan couldn't quite keep a smile of pride off her face.

"In charge!" Ziegler repeated, half teasingly, half in congratulations.

"Shut up," said Tan. "Let's start roll call."

Roll call was very brief, and it was only a few minutes later that Benno was heading toward the exit to start his patrol—when he glanced out the window.

His glance coincided with the exact moment that a certain car drove by. A patrol car. A patrol car in which he recognized the driver.

It was Deputy Derrick.

Benno froze.

An alarm bell rang in the back of his head.

He darted back toward the bull pen. "Tan!" he called. "Did Grogan pull Derrick off watch duty at the hospital?"

"What are you talking about?"

"Derrick just drove by. No one's watching over Browning!"

With an air of cool efficiency, Tan went straight to a radio terminal and activated a microphone on the console. "Deputy Derrick, do you copy? This is the station calling Derrick. Do you copy? Over." She glanced at Benno. "Could Pressler be messing with our radios again?"

"Try the sheriff."

"Station calling Sheriff Grogan. Do you copy? Sheriff Grogan, can you hear me?"

Finally a response came. *"Station, this is Ziegler. I just started my patrol. Is everything all right?"*

"No," said Benno, though Ziegler couldn't hear him. "Something's very wrong."

"Get to the mayor's office," said Tan. "Tell Grogan what's going on." As Benno hurried off, Tan spoke into the microphone: "Ziegler, meet me at the hospital."

Benno sped to the mayor's office on Main Street. As he raced from his patrol car to the building's front entrance, he glimpsed Sheriff Grogan and Violet through a window; they were just entering the main office. Mayor Pressler stood up from his desk to greet them, his back to the window.

Then a fourth person entered the room, and Benno stopped short.

It was Wade Browning.

In a flash, Browning caught Violet from behind and held a knife to her throat.

VII

Mayor Pressler never thought he would find himself missing Sheriff Dubowski. All those months of scheming, the two of them being thorns in each other's sides, and then, just one day—*one* day—after Pressler finally brought his rival under his control, Dubowski had to go and get himself killed. Now he'd have to start all over again with the new sheriff, though thankfully, so far, Grogan hadn't been much of a pain. Not nearly as much as Violet, anyway.

However, for the first time since Halloween night, Pressler was no longer preoccupied with Violet. In fact, she hardly mattered to him anymore, though he still needed to find out about this Wade Browning and who had really hired him, and why. Pressler had plans for Veil, and he couldn't have outside elements complicating his business affairs. That was why he wished Dubowski were here now, to deal with all of that while Pressler turned his thoughts toward…this other problem.

Mirror, mirror...

How had he missed this?! That night in November, when the body of Rob Mulroy had turned up in the deputy's car alongside one of the serial killer's victims, Pressler had of course had his suspicions. But he'd checked on that! He'd made absolutely sure!

Or had he? He knew, after all, that an accomplice was involved. And accomplices were useful for creating alibis, as he knew too well. But even so—*those* two? Working together?! The very idea was absurd! Or so he'd thought. Of course, they did technically have one connection...

The trouble was, even if he was right, if he voiced his suspicions—publicly or anonymously—somehow, eventually, it would lead back to him! He had to keep it secret for now, all of it. But something would have to be done. He did not have the leverage he'd thought he had. He did not have control. Those he could not control were dangerous.

Those he could not control had to be eliminated.

"Mr. Mayor?" His secretary's voice issued from the intercom on his desk. *"Sheriff Grogan is here to see you—with Violet."*

Speaking of, he thought. "Send them in."

He stood up to greet them, a mark of just how much had changed between him and these people in a short space of time. Only two days ago, if they'd paid him a visit, he'd have received them sitting down, behind his desk, as an expression of power. Standing up was reflexive, standard for greeting an ordinary visitor. That's what they were to him now—ordinary. And he, to them, was simply a politician.

He wondered if they'd notice the change.

"Sheriff Grogan," he said heartily. "And Violet Grogan as well. I'd heard you acquired a surname. I hope you'll accept my congratulations."

After a moment, Violet gave him an icy smile. "Thank you."

He turned back to Jen Grogan. "So, to what do I owe this unexpected pleasure?"

With a scowl, Grogan said, "Did you really think I'd let Violet come see you alone?"

Pressler looked back and forth between her and Violet. To the latter he said, "I'm sorry, did we have an appointment?"

The sheriff gave an exasperated sigh. "You called her a few minutes ago, asking her to come here."

"Well, not him, his office," Violet corrected her before Pressler could protest. "I assumed it was a secretary."

"You mean Brenda?" asked Pressler.

Violet glanced back toward the outer office. "No, it wasn't Brenda."

Pressler frowned. "Then it seems you're the victim of a prank."

"Uh-huh." Grogan turned to Violet and jerked her head toward the door, then started to lead the way out. Violet looked from her to Pressler uncertainly.

"Well, wait a minute." Pressler held up a hand. "What did the person say, exactly?"

Before they could answer, the door opened again. Both women were looking at Pressler, so neither of them saw it. Pressler wondered peripherally how someone could be entering without Brenda having announced them.

What happened next was incredible. Wade Browning appeared, wearing hospital scrubs under an expensive-looking coat, as if he'd burgled a doctor's private office. But how could he be here? He was still unconscious in the hospital. He had to be! Otherwise Penny, the nurse who acted as Pressler's spy, would have contacted him and told him...

The coldness in Browning's eyes ought to have been a warning. When he snaked his arm around Violet's chest and tickled her throat with a glinting blade, she gave a shriek. He quickly shushed her. "Let's all stay calm," he said in a would-be soothing voice, looking pointedly at the sheriff. Holding Violet in front of him, he pivoted toward Pressler. "Mr. Mayor? If you wouldn't mind stepping out from behind your desk, so I know you're not doing anything you shouldn't?"

Pressler's hand had been reaching toward a certain button hidden from view. With Browning watching him like a hawk, the mayor stood up slowly and complied.

Browning—and Violet—pivoted back to Grogan. "Your sidearm, if you wouldn't mind, Sheriff."

Grogan unholstered her weapon and, using a finger and thumb, set it on the ground and slid it over to him using her foot.

"Now," said Browning in a sighing voice, "perhaps you would be so kind as to tell me—*which one of you tried to kill me?*"

There was a moment of bemused silence.

"It wasn't us!" squeaked Violet. "We didn't do it!"

"We've been trying to find out who attacked you," Grogan told him, speaking slowly and clearly. "The problem is, we have so little information to go on. Why don't you let her go, and you can help us fill in the blanks? You could start by telling us who you really are and how you were attacked."

Browning sneered at her. "Something tells me you already know the answer to both."

"Not specifically," chimed in Pressler, "but we can guess. You're a private investigator, aren't you? Do you seriously believe that town officials would conspire to commit murder? Don't you think it's more likely that your would-be assailant is someone who followed you here? Some enemy of *yours?*"

Browning snickered. He put his mouth to Violet's ear. "Got the mayor on a leash, huh?"

Though trembling and panting, Violet managed to throw him a quizzical look. "What?"

"During our get-to-know-you dinners, you mentioned how

corrupt and criminal the mayor is. I knew that meant he must be an ally of yours."

Violet rolled her eyes.

"You haven't answered my question," Pressler said acidly.

"No," drawled Browning, "I don't think some shadowy enemy showed up out of my past to take me out just when it's most convenient for you all."

"Well," said Grogan, "maybe it wasn't someone from your past! Maybe it was—the person who hired you for this job!"

A frantic look appeared in Violet's eyes. "Jen—"

"Violet, I know it isn't the man you lived with who's after you. If you won't tell me who it is you're really afraid of, maybe he can." She looked at Browning. "So who hired you?"

Browning hesitated.

He hesitated so long that Pressler answered for him: "Of course. He doesn't know."

Browning threw him a baleful look.

"He was hired anonymously. They paid him something up front and promised him the rest when he delivered."

"Think you're pretty smart, huh?" Browning tightened his grip around Violet, causing her to whimper. "Tell me this, then—why would my client try to kill me?"

At first no one had an answer for him, then—

"Because they don't need you anymore," whispered Violet.

"What?"

"They don't need you anymore now that you've found me."

Browning brought the tip of his knife to her cheekbone. She shook, gasping. "Tell me who 'they' are," he ordered.

At that moment, Pressler saw a shadow slowly forming in the door behind Browning and Violet. The shadow resolved itself into Deputy Benno, silently approaching.

With an infinitesimal turn of his head, Pressler saw that Sheriff Grogan had also noticed the slowly creeping deputy. Her eyes had gone very wide.

"Tell me!" Browning repeated.

As Benno started to cross the threshold, his eyes went to the sheriff, who gave an almost imperceptible shake of the head. Her hand, though she kept it lowered at her side, stretched out its fingers and made several sideways, pushing motions. *Keep back!* she was telling him. *Keep out of it!*

Benno paused, then reluctantly retreated, quietly slipping out of view.

"I said, tell me!!"

"All right! All right," Violet sobbed. She gulped. "I...I don't know what they're called, but...there's an organization that..." She tried to turn her head to look at Browning. "You're not going to believe me—"

"TELL ME!!!"

"It's an organization of people who think they know who should have—have extraordinary gifts and talents—and—and who shouldn't. Like, if they find someone who's really fast or strong, and they don't think that person should have that, they'll—they'll paralyze that person, or worse!"

"What do you mean?" asked Browning. "How do they decide who's...who's—"

"Unfit," provided Violet.

"Like, are they secret Nazis?"

"I don't—"

"Are you unfit if you're not Christian? Not Republican?"

"I don't know!"

"Not white? Not straight?"

"I don't know!"

"Well, pick one!" Browning's tone was mocking. "There are plenty of clichés available. You've gotta add detail to make it more convincing!"

"I told you you wouldn't—"

"Because you're a bad liar! This 'organization' doesn't exist, and the person who tried to kill me is in this room."

They found me! Violet wailed. "Last fall, I noticed a man watching me, following me. I lost him. Then there was another man. I ran and I ran, but they finally caught up with me at a cabin a few miles from here. They trapped me. One of them told me I was 'unfit' to have a perfect memory. I—I blew up the propane tank—"

"Yeah, cool origin story. I'm sure I saw a movie once with the same plot."

"That's why I'm worried about Megan!"

"Who?"

"Megan Toombs!" Violet looked appealingly at Grogan. "She was just recognized as a math prodigy! If she gets on their radar because of me—"

"All right, enough already!" hollered Browning. "I'm not buying this, you understand?"

"Maybe some of it is a lie," said Pressler, staring curiously at Violet, "but what if some of it is true? How do you know for sure your clients wouldn't rather dispose of you than have to pay you, now that you've found her?"

"Because that wasn't my job!" snarled Browning. In answer to Violet's look of confusion, he whispered, "That's right. That's how I know your story's a lie. The way you tell it, this organization knew about you and your memory before you went under the radar, and then lost you or thought you were dead. But my client had never *heard* of you until after you'd turned up here in Veil. They wanted me to find out your real name."

After a moment or two of perplexity, Violet stammered, "That's because they're not sure I'm the same person they were after. There were no photographs of me from before—"

"But they were tailing you!"

"Excuse me," interrupted Pressler. "I'm afraid I'm having a hard time following all of this, but it sounds like Violet's real name is your true goal."

"You think I'm lying?!" snapped Browning.

"Therefore, if we were to give you the name, would you let us go?"

Browning seemed taken aback by this, and somewhat suspicious. "Maybe."

"Well?" Pressler gestured toward Sheriff Grogan.

The sheriff looked troubled. To Browning she said, "Let her go first."

Browning chuckled. "I don't think so."

"Please," sobbed Violet.

"First tell me your name!"

"You're gonna kill me…"

"Just let her go, and we can talk!" Grogan implored.

"Your NAME!"

"Please!"

"Oh, for God's sake, *I'll* tell you!!" Pressler pointed at Violet. "Her real name is Katie Wilner."

The three other people in the room went silent, wearing stunned expressions.

"She's wanted for aggravated assault in Mayville, New York. You can look up her records. *Katie—Wilner.*"

"How do you know that?" asked Browning.

"Doesn't matter. Now I suggest you put down the weapon and cooperate. If your client's really that desperate for the name, you can use it as leverage to force them to help you out of the legal mess you're about to be in."

Pressler waited, curious to see how his gamble would pay off. Everyone in the office was still...

And then something truly bizarre happened.

Wade Browning lowered the knife from Violet's throat—not warily, but in a manner that was completely casual. And Violet—rather than bolting to escape the clutches of her captor—remained where she was with an expression of bewildered dismay. "Katie Wilner," she repeated softly.

"Which one was that?" Wade Browning asked in a tone of voice completely different from before. He sounded concerned, friendly even.

"That was Deputy Tan," the sheriff murmured grimly.

Violet looked at her and shook her head. "It can't be."

Pressler looked at each of them in turn, in growing befuddlement. "What—what's—what is this? What's happening?"

Footsteps approached.

"Stand down, Deputy!" Sheriff Grogan held up a hand, and Benno halted just inside the door. "It's all right!" she told him. "The situation's stable."

Wade Browning pointed at Benno. "How long has *he* been here?"

Pressler lost his patience. "What the hell—?!"

"Mr. Mayor," said Grogan, "I'd like you to meet someone." She laid a hand on Wade Browning's shoulder. "This is Tony Ledbetter. He's an actor."

Benno did a double take.

Violet threw the deputy a guilty look.

The sheriff went on, "I hired Tony to help me find out which one of my deputies was spying on us for you."

VIII

"I don't understand!" swore Deputy Tan—and it really sounded as though she didn't.

Standing on the other side of her desk, Sheriff Grogan glanced at Deputy Benno. "I'd hoped to explain it to all the deputies at once," she said ruefully, "but maybe it's better this way." She took a deep breath.

The second before she began, Benno threw a glance at Violet, standing in the corner. She looked as if she wished she were anywhere but here.

"Throughout our attempts over the last few months to expose Elijah Pressler as a criminal and bring him to justice, he's always been one step ahead of us. With Violet's help, I found evidence that he must be spying on us here in the department. I endeavored to learn how. I discovered he has spies placed strategically throughout Veil—the hospital, the bank, the post office, even the school. From that, I concluded he must also have a spy in this department."

"And you think it's me?!"

If Grogan was at all moved by the hurt in Tan's voice, she didn't show it. She went on, "I saw this as a rare opportunity. I set myself two goals: to discover the spy's identity, and to use that discovery, if I could, to bring the crime home to Pressler."

Violet opened her mouth to say something, then hesitated.

"To do this," continued Grogan, "I needed a scenario involving a distraction, a set of circumstances to manipulate Pressler into outing himself without him realizing that was what he was doing." She glanced at Violet. "We threw around dozens of scenarios till we settled on one in which a grifter would pose as someone from Violet's past. I called Tony Ledbetter, and last week we set the plan in motion, with him playing the part of Wade Browning."

"That's how he faked the photos of him and Violet," realized Benno, "because they really *were* of him and Violet. But how did you get rid of the scar?" He pointed at his forehead.

"Cy has a computer program," Violet said softly.

"No wonder I couldn't find anything on social media," murmured Deputy Tan. Then she frowned. "Wait a minute. You couldn't have faked *all* the stuff we dug up on Browning. We spoke to the hospital, to the county police department... Or *you* did." She pointed accusingly at Benno. "Were you in on this? Were you lying when you said you—"

"Deputy Benno was not privy to the plan," Grogan interrupted.

"Then how could they have told him those things?"

"We informed the hospital and the police department of what we were doing and asked them to cooperate."

Both Tan and Benno wore frowns of disbelief. "They just agreed to that?" said Benno doubtfully. "I can't believe they would ever do that, even for fellow officers. They don't just get involved in other departments' affairs."

"We had some help convincing them," Grogan explained. "As Veil's senior deputy for almost thirty years, Hal Clayton has friends in practically every town in New England. He called in some long-standing favors. In fact, Wade Browning's entire character history was built around where those favors could be called in."

Tan, who had known Hal longer than any of the others in the room, asked, "Why would Hal agree to be part of this?"

For the first time, the sheriff showed signs of discomfiture. Violet came to her rescue. "Hal, um... He said I could share this—he suspected Keith Dubowski of being the attempted rapist—I think it had to do with something back when he knew Dubowski before he was sheriff—but he never said anything, so he blamed himself for what happened to Bethany and Joy and me. He wanted to make up for it."

Benno shook his head. "But even with other cops cooperating, you still couldn't have faked the birth certificate or the death certificate or the other things Derrick found!"

"Deputy Derrick *was* privy to the plan."

Benno received this news in stony silence.

"Of course, all the evidence we manufactured was circumstantial. There was nothing to confirm that what 'Wade' said about being Violet's stepfather was true, which was exactly what we were going for. We wanted Pressler and his spy to be suspicious of Browning, not of *us*."

Tan turned to Violet. "So you really don't have your memories back."

Benno looked at her sharply. "How do you know about that?!"

Tan turned to him in confusion. "Violet told me last night, when I found her staking out the Toombs place."

Benno turned slowly to Violet, dawning realization in his eyes. Violet couldn't meet his gaze.

Doing a double take, Tan said, "Wait—how do *you* know about that?"

"Because," said Grogan, "what happened last night between you and Violet also happened between Violet and Benno. In fact, she had to repeat the scene with *all* of the deputies—just as she had to stage an incident after each dinner with Wade, in front of a different deputy each time. All of you were led to believe that Violet had gotten her memories back, and that some mysterious danger from her past was threatening her. You also each believed you were the only deputy who knew about it. The only variation on the story was Violet's former name, a different name given to each deputy."

"I searched the name she gave me," remarked Benno. "I found a police report on her."

"Me, too," said Tan. "It said Katie Wilner was wanted for aggravated assault against a man who'd been accused of sexual harassment but never charged."

Grogan nodded. "It was…disturbingly easy to find so many reports that fit the same general description. We just had to pick out the ones that lacked photographs."

"So there really is a Stephanie Newcombe," said Benno.

"Yes," said Violet without facing them.

"And then," said Grogan, "the last phase: the three of us staging a hostage situation in front of Pressler—though we didn't count on someone going above and beyond the call of duty, and almost blowing it." She regarded Benno with wry amusement.

Benno tried not to sound defensive as he explained, "I saw Derrick drive by when he was supposed to be guarding Wade Browning. I guess now we know why he wasn't."

"Yes, we needed him to distract Pressler's secretary so Tony could slip into the mayor's office unnoticed."

"What about the break-in at the coroner's office?" asked Benno. "How did that fit into this?"

Grogan blinked at him in surprise. "That wasn't part of our plan," she said, "that was a real break-in."

"But I still don't understand!" Tan protested. "Why did you need to stage a hostage situation in front of Pressler?"

The sheriff's grim demeanor returned. "We had to force him into a scenario where he'd have to give Violet's true name, a name he could only know if his spy had passed it on to him."

"I'm not Pressler's spy!!"

"He gave the name Katie Wilner. Violet and I kept the names we chose strictly between the two of us. The only other person who had ever heard that name was you."

"But you know me!" insisted Tan. "You know I would never spy on you for him! I want to bring him down just as much as you do! This is my job—no, it's more than my job, it's my *life!* If I betrayed you guys, I'd be betraying *myself!*" She looked appealingly at Benno, but he seemed lost in uncertainty. She turned pleadingly back to Grogan. "Sheriff…"

Jen Grogan's eyes held grim resignation. She drew breath to speak.

"Jen," said Violet, turning around, "I think she's telling the truth."

"How is that possible?" The sheriff didn't quite manage to keep hope out of her voice.

"I don't know…but I keep thinking of what Pressler said to me when we were in his office."

"What did he say?" asked Benno.

"He congratulated me on having 'acquired' a surname. How could he have known about that?"

"Wasn't that to do with the article in the *Chronicle* that you were interviewed for?" asked Grogan.

"But that article hasn't come out yet! The only time I ever

mentioned it was to you, here in this office…" Violet stared off into space, a startled look in her eye. With a gasp she pointed at Tan. "You brought me here!"

"What??"

"Benno and all the other deputies sat and talked with me in the car, but you were the only one who made me drive with you to the station—and we talked here, in this office!" Abruptly, without a word of explanation, she began to dart about the room, peering behind filing cabinets, behind window shades, under chairs.

Nonplussed, Benno and Tan moved repeatedly out of her way.

"Violet, what are you looking for?" asked Grogan.

Violet froze, her fingers groping the leg of the desk where it met the floor. She strained for a moment, grunted, then rose and held out an object on her palm. "This."

Grogan took the object, mesmerized. "Holy…"

"There was never a spy in the department. Pressler bugged the station."

* * *

They found five bugs in all when they searched the building. Knowing he used to work for a security company, the sheriff asked Deputy Ziegler to examine them. Ziegler was notably less talkative and more sullen than usual, but he carried out the task with every sign of professionalism.

He reported that the bugs were of a kind that sent signals to a short-range receiver. The next logical step in the investigation would be to search Pressler's properties for the receiver, but to do that they'd need a warrant. To procure a warrant could take up to several days.

However, luck seemed to favor the sheriff's efforts. Deputy

Trent called in during his patrol and reported that the front door of Pressler's residence was standing ajar. Eleven-year-old Megan Toombs, who had been in her front yard in a booth, selling Girl Scout cookies since Pressler had left for work that morning, would eventually serve as a witness that no one had gone up to Pressler's door all that morning. The deputies took advantage of the fortuitous opportunity, and they were rewarded: they found absolutely no trace of the receiver whatsoever. If they had found it, something would be very wrong, for Pressler would never keep an item so incriminating in his own home. Strangely they couldn't find any sign that the house had been broken into, but this served them even further: if someone had entered the house with a key, signifying premeditation, then that was enough probable cause to search Pressler's other properties, in case someone might have tried to illegally enter one of them, too.

They found the receiver in the fourth property they searched, in the back office of what was once a bowling alley. It was brought to the station, where Ziegler explained how someone could download the recorded conversations and then send them to Pressler or hand them off to him.

He also said that there were some recordings still within the receiver, but that there were six sets, not five. Somewhere, one bug had yet to be found.

* * *

After locking the door to the area with the jail cells, Deputy Benno turned—and found Violet standing a few doors down the station hallway. She had a timid look on her face, as if he'd caught her doing something wrong. Benno reflected on how wildly he'd misinterpreted her guilty expressions the last few days.

She gave a shy, awkward wave.

Benno had spent part of the day thinking about two conversations he would have to have. He realized this was the moment he must decide how to go about one of them.

Violet started to turn away.

"Violet," called Benno.

"Yes?"

He went over to her. She swallowed nervously but stood her ground.

"I need to ask you something."

"Yes! Sure! Of course."

"Last night, the reason you were parked so far from the Toombs house was so that Pressler wouldn't happen to look out his front window and see you. Was that it?"

"That's right," stammered Violet. "If he'd seen me talking to all the deputies in a row, he might have caught on."

"Right. And I was the last deputy you…spoke to?"

"Mm-hm." Violet suddenly seemed very interested in her shoes.

"Well, no wonder you were exhausted."

Relief at his understanding flashed across the young woman's face, though she didn't look up.

"One more question, and I really need you to be honest with me on this one."

She nodded quickly, tensing.

"Is Trisha a good kisser?"

Violet's head came straight up. "What?!"

"I mean, I'd rate her, like, an eight, but I'd love to know what you'd give her."

Very slowly a smile spread across Violet's face. "Are you— teasing me?"

Benno's face also broke out into a grin. He pulled a watery-eyed Violet into a gentle hug. For a long moment they held each other.

"I almost told you, that one time, what we were doing," Violet said.

"You must be glad this week is over."

He could physically feel the tension disperse from her small shoulders. "You have no idea." She pulled away and added, "It didn't really work the way we thought it would, but at least we finally got him."

Benno glanced back toward the cells. "Well, Sheriff doesn't want to formally charge him with illegal surveillance until we find all the bugs. She wants the case against him to be as airtight as possible. If we end up finding that last bug later in a completely different location, his defense could use it as evidence. My guess is, we're not going to find it, so we'll have to release him in an hour or so."

Thinking a moment, Violet asked, "Benno, could you do me a favor?"

"Name it."

* * *

Pressler picked at the food that Deputy Benno had just brought him. It didn't look quite as inedible as he'd expected. He had a bite almost to his mouth when the jail door opened again. The deputy was back, this time with company.

Seeing who it was, Pressler let the food drop back onto the plate and gave a lopsided grin. "Well. I would've thought gloating was beneath you, but I guess I was wrong."

Violet's expression was neutral but steady. She came up to within a few feet of the bars of the cell.

"I've got to hand it to you," Pressler said in an oily voice, "this was some first-class chicanery. Fooling me is not easy, but you..." He gave a chef's kiss. "You're a much better liar than I ever gave you credit for, Miss Grogan. Tell me—how did it feel, saying those lies over and over again?"

He waited for a twitch in her jaw, a pulsing vein in her forehead, some sign that keeping a poker-face was costing her effort, but Violet looked as if she were simply bored.

"How did it feel," he pressed, "deceiving all those people you knew were allies—just to catch little old me?" He glanced at Benno. "If I were you, I'd be worried the deputies might never trust me again, now that they know how good a liar I am. And what about the rest of Veil? You want to rebuild their trust in the deputies, but now it turns out that the sheriff, herself, doesn't trust them?" He grabbed the cage and brought his face between two of the bars. "Was catching me really worth all of that?"

"I want to talk to you about something," said Violet.

Pressler chuckled. "Don't have an answer for me, eh?"

A brief pause, then she repeated, almost mechanically, "I want to talk to you about something."

Still chuckling, Pressler sat back down and picked up the plate again.

"I want to talk to you about Rob Mulroy."

The plate clattered to the floor, sending food everywhere.

Pressler didn't say anything. He stared at Violet as blankly as he could.

"I want to tell you about something he did to Cy while they were dating," said Violet. "Cy said I could share it with you. Occasionally she'd call him out for something, or just let him know that something he said or did hurt her. Sometimes she'd just want to talk, come up with a plan to do things differently so they'd both feel comfortable, so they could both give consent. But every time she tried, he'd make *such a big stink*—she was making a big deal out of nothing, she should accept him the way he is or break up with him, she was the *only* girl in the entire world who was bothered by—"

"Okay, I get it!"

"No. You don't. He did what too many boyfriends do: make it *so exhausting* to ever have an adult conversation that the girlfriend won't even try in the future. And that kind of thing doesn't just happen between romantic couples."

"Look," interrupted Pressler, "I never tried to manipulate Cyanne. I don't know what she told you, but I never wanted anything from her. Believe it or not, I genuinely care about her."

"But you *did* want something from her—the same things she gave me: friendship and the chance to be human."

Pressler scoffed. "Is that what this is? An attempt to reform me? Are you gonna tell me there's 'still good in me?' Or that it's 'not too late to change?'"

"Would you rather she threatened you?" asked Deputy Benno with a raised eyebrow. "We already know you're scared of her."

Before Pressler could reply, Violet raised her voice: "I didn't come to try to scare you or reform you. You and I both know you're not a good man—in fact, I think knowing it gives you a feeling of power, of freedom. But I also know you think you're above it all, that something separates you from 'ordinary criminals.'" She paused for breath, then said, "What you tried to do to me—get me to leave you alone by messing with my family—is no different from what Cy's ex did to her. That's what I came to tell you…you're just another Rob Mulroy."

Slowly Pressler rose to his feet. He stared at Violet with such intense, smoldering fury as he had never felt before. If not for the bars, he might have leapt at her then and there. Benno seemed to sense this, as he stepped unnecessarily to the woman's side.

Violet gazed up steadily at Pressler. "I'm never going to stop fighting you," she said. "You can try all the gaslighting you want. You don't control me. And every time you try, you can count on me to remind you of who you really are." She turned to leave.

"That's rich, coming from someone who doesn't even know who *she* is," snarled Pressler.

She pivoted back. "I am every person in the world who is *DONE* with toxic men like you. Pleased to meet you."

And with that she was gone.

IX

J en made minute adjustments to the receiver, one after
another. Ziegler had shown her how to work the controls,
but no matter how she fiddled with it, she couldn't coax
any sound out of it. Grudgingly, she accepted the obvious
conclusion: there just wasn't any sound to pick up on the other
end. Wherever the last bug was hidden, no one and nothing
was making any noise. Which meant that the last bug was *not*
at the sheriff's station.

She slumped against the back of her chair. Where the conflict
with Pressler was concerned, they still had a ways to go.

A tap at her door made her look up.

"Hi," said Tony Ledbetter. He wore some of the clothes he'd
used to embody the part of Wade Browning, though now he'd
donned a denim jacket and a worn Red Sox baseball cap.

"Tony," said Jen. Her breath caught, and in a slightly different
tone she said, "Mr. Ledbetter, I didn't know you were still here."

'Well, I was just, um…" After a moment, he apparently decided
he had no further use for that sentence, and tossed it aside with
a jerk of his head. "Would you like to go out for a drink?"

Without displaying an inordinate amount of alarm, Jen moved
swiftly to the door, pulled the man inside, and shut it. "Look,

Tony…I don't know how you normally do things after a one-night stand, but—"

"Actually you were my first," Tony said cheerfully. "Buhhht I'm sensing this is a no."

"It's a no."

"Got it." He opened the door, still cheerful, albeit resigned.

He was almost to the exit when Jen called from her office, "Mr. Ledbetter?"

"Yeah?"

"Thanks. For everything."

Tony tipped his baseball cap and disappeared.

Jen gave a mighty stretch. It was late, and she'd been at it the whole day. There was one more thing she had to do before she left. With a deep sigh, she headed toward the jail cells.

She took what satisfaction she could from the sight that greeted her when she opened the door to the cell area: Pressler was standing with his hands on the bars, beadily watching the door. He was clearly more than ready to leave.

"Elijah Pressler," she said, deadpan, "by the laws governing this town, I am not permitted to hold you more than twelve hours without filing formal charges against you. However, this is an ongoing investigation and you are still a person of interest, so I must ask you not to leave Veil until the investigation is complete. Do you understand?"

To Jen's surprise, he contained his answer to a simple, "Yes, I understand."

It wasn't like Pressler to pass up an opportunity for a taunt. She pulled a set of keys from her pocket and as she looked for the one she needed, she counted off the seconds in her head, betting herself she wouldn't get past eight. She'd gotten to five when he spoke again, "Ironic, isn't it. Getting me out of Veil is your real goal, yet here you are, telling me I have to stay... Has it ever occurred to you how alike we are?"

Jen raised a quizzical eyebrow.

"I grew up in Veil, just like you," he went on. "As an adult, I left, started my life elsewhere, but when things got complicated—dangerous, hostile—I came back, just as you did."

"I came back to Veil because I thought it was the best thing for Cyanne." She found the right key and stepped toward the cell door. "You came back because you wanted to make Veil part of your criminal enterprise."

"Is that what Dubowski told you?"

The key was almost to the lock. Jen froze.

Her eyes found Pressler's. Something in the way she looked at him made his bluster drain away.

"Did you know?" she asked softly.

"Did I know what?"

"Did you know that it was Dubowski who abducted and tried to rape that poor woman?"

Pressler shrugged casually. "Will it matter what I say? Seems you've made up your mind already."

"I always thought it was unlikely how she managed to escape from him. He was twice her size and had plenty of experience keeping prisoners in custody. But if she had help...if you sent one of your henchmen to save her without her or Dubowski knowing..."

Pressler groaned. "I can tell exactly where this conversation is going. First I answer your question: 'Maybe I did.' And you tell me: 'Saving her doesn't make you a hero, Mr. Mayor. You only did it to gain leverage over the sheriff. You acted out of selfishness. Well, you won't find it so easy to get leverage over me!' Is that close to what you were going to say?"

Jen tilted her head curiously. "Did Violet come and talk to you?"

Pressler was thrown. "Why do you ask?"

Jen shrugged. "Maybe all I was going to say was, 'Thank you for doing what you did, even if it was for the wrong reason.'" She unlocked and opened the cell door.

Pressler stared at her dubiously. "Is that *really* all you want to say to me?"

"It's all I'm going to." She gestured for him to take his leave.

Shrugging her off, Pressler strode past her, as if leaving behind a nuisance. As he neared the door to the hallway, he slowed, paused, and for a moment it seemed he was turning back to her. Perhaps there was something more that *he* wanted to say.

Whatever it was, it went unsaid. The door creaked, and he was gone.

Jen tiredly eyed the mess on the floor of the cell. Grabbing a broom and dustpan, she swept most of it up and made a mental note to take care of the rest in the morning.

Returning to her office, Jen glimpsed a shadow through the door. "Violet? Oh." She found Deputy Benno standing by the desk. "Benno, I thought you'd gone home."

Benno stared at her a moment without saying anything, then he motioned with his head to the receiver. "Anything?"

"No, nothing. Wherever the last bug is, it's not in the station. Which at least means the station is bug-free."

"Hm... Does that mean it was worth it? Staging all of this?"

Jen gave him a steady look. "Yes," she said. "I'd say it was."

Benno nodded very slowly. "You were all very convincing," he said without inflection. "You and Cy and Violet."

"This week was incredibly difficult for Violet. I hope you're not holding anything against her."

"Violet and I are cool."

Jen heard the slight emphasis on Violet's name. She stepped directly in front of her deputy. "Benno, is there something you need to say?"

Benno appeared to be focused on something over her left shoulder.

"I knew," she went on, "when I decided to do this there would be hurt feelings. That's why I wanted to explain to all of you, at the same time, why I—"

"Who are you?"

"Come again?"

Benno looked her full in the face. "Who are you and what have you done with Jen Grogan? With the woman I respected and looked up to?"

Jen had never seen him so angry and hurt, and she was very much taken aback. She took the time to carefully form a reply. "I was wrong about there being a spy in the department. But all the evidence at the time indicated otherwise. I did what I thought was right, although, for what it's worth, I couldn't believe any of the deputies could be working for Pressler. Thank God I was right about that—"

"Derrick."

"Pardon?"

"You tested all the deputies *except Derrick*."

Jen put her fingertips together and bowed till they touched her forehead, as if praying for patience. "Put yourself in my place, Benno. I had to consider the possibility that someone in the department—someone I've worked with and trusted with my *life*—might be spying on us for a dangerous criminal. I had to put my personal feelings aside and look at the situation coolly and logically. Derrick was devoted to Dubowski, so I couldn't

86

see any way that Pressler might be controlling him. And we needed—"

"But he might be controlling the rest of us?! Derrick, of all people, gets your trust because of his blind loyalty to the sheriff?!"

"As I said, he was loyal to *Dubowski*. He has no special loyalty to me."

"Wrong. Since your little test, I'm pretty sure, by default, Derrick's the most loyal deputy you've got."

Jen looked away, stung. Reining in her temper, she said in a low voice, "You're probably right. It was a tough decision I didn't want to have to make. I hope someday you all give me a chance to earn back your trust."

"Earn back—?! Ma'am, what you did was *wrong*. With the facts—"

"It's not your job to decide that, Deputy!"

"With the facts you had, the right thing would've been for you to *talk* to us, to tell us what the evidence showed. Tell us you couldn't believe it to be true, but you were obligated to *ask!* I know you wanted to get back at Pressler for trying to split up you and Cy, but—"

"Stop right there, Benno," Jen snapped. "That's going too far."

"No, ma'am, *you* went too far. I don't think you realize the damage you've done."

"You want to talk about damage?! Imagine if I'd done what you suggested just now. Would we ever have found out about the bugs in the station? We've *proven* that there's no spy, but if we hadn't, and if the town got wind that Pressler might be spying on us through one of the deputies... Well, do you think they'd ever trust us?! They barely trust us now! It would be chaos! Every time we'd try to help, they'd be watching us like feral animals, wondering which of us is going to turn out to be another Hayden! I had to—"

"No." Benno shook his head at her in appalled dismay. "No, you did not just say that."

Jen didn't know what he was talking about. "Benno," she said through clenched teeth, "I'm being very patient. I know I asked you if you had something to say, but this—"

"Hayden is still one of us!"

"What??"

"She's still part of our team."

Jen gaped at him. "Benno, she tried to murder an innocent woman!"

"No. I read your report. She *threatened* to murder an innocent woman. She was subdued before she had a chance to carry out that threat. For all we know, she might have come to her senses before she crossed the line."

"I hope you're not saying we shouldn't have stopped her."

"Of course not. And I'm not minimalizing the harm she did."

"It kind of sounds like you are."

"Jen, she made a *mistake!* A *terrible* mistake! We're all capable of making them! Yes, she betrayed us, betrayed her badge, betrayed the people she swore to protect, and she needs to face the consequences. But if we just abandon her, how is she going to come back from it?"

Jen stared at him like he'd grown a second head. "Benno, there *is* no coming back from it! It's not a crime to want to do someone harm, but once she acted on those thoughts she lost her place in this community. She's not part of it anymore."

Benno seemed so dumbfounded he could no longer look at her. "If that's really what you think, then you're not fit to wear that badge."

A chilly silence met this remark. The tension within it grew the longer it lasted. It might have been a relief to them both if Jen had simply shouted at Benno to get out. Instead she spoke softly. "Would you rather Dubowski were still wearing it? Or was the crime he committed just another 'mistake?' Should we have defended him, covered it up, painted his victims as liars? If he were still alive, would he be 'still part of the team?'"

Benno spoke just as quietly, still not looking at her. It almost sounded as if he were speaking to himself. "What Dubowski did shows he was never really one of us to begin with. He was irredeemable. Hayden was in love with him. When he died and his crimes came to light, she was in shock—more so than the rest of us. We had each other to talk to and start processing it all, but…" He looked at Jen. "But *you sent her home.* She had no one. When she decided to kill Joy Dosley, she thought she was doing the right thing. She had no idea…*but she knows now.* What she doesn't know is how to move on. Just like before, she has no one to help her." He looked away again. "And now the rest of us know, when one of us makes a mistake…you won't be there for us either."

By this point, Jen, too, had lost the ability to look him in the eye. She spoke in a deadly whisper she'd never used with anyone before: *"You can go."*

Benno went. Just before he passed out of the building, Jen heard him say something that sounded like, "Pam was right."

X

"**M**om? Are you okay?"

Cy and Violet had just had dinner at their favorite café, and they'd stopped by the sheriff's station on the way home. Jen did not look okay, thought Violet as she and Cy approached her office. The sheriff of Veil looked perturbed, even haunted, standing there, staring fixedly at nothing.

With a start, Jen came out of her reverie and said distractedly, "Yeah, I'm fine. I—just need a good night's sleep."

"We brought you some leftovers." Violet proffered a to-go box.

Jen gave a wan smile. "You two are sweet. Why don't you bring that home and put it in the fridge? I won't be long. I just have to—" She broke off at an abrupt smattering of sound from the electronic equipment on the desk. Jen darted to the other side and began adjusting the controls.

"What is that?" asked Cy.

"That's the receiver for the bugs Pressler planted in the station," Violet told her. "It's what he used to listen in."

"Shh!" Jen waved at them to be quiet.

They heard some mechanical clicks, then a creak, like a door opening. There was a muffled *thud*, then a series of footsteps;

those, too, seemed muffled. After a minute, there came a *thump*, then a tearing, ripping sound, and suddenly the noises were muffled no longer.

"There's a voice," whispered Cy.

Jen held up a hand. Her daughter was right. There was a man's voice, a low constant muttering. Jen grimaced and turned to Violet. "Can you make out what he's saying?"

Violet closed her eyes and strained her hearing. "'Wall,' I think he said, 'Wall.' There, he said it again."

"Sounded like 'Saul' to me," said Cy.

A violent sneeze made all three of them do a double take.

"Is that…"

"Pressler?!"

A coarse invective left them without any doubt.

"The last bug is in his house," Violet realized wonderingly.

"I'm going over there," said Jen. She started to put on her coat.

"But that doesn't make any sense!" Cy protested. "Why would he bug himself?"

A glint of light caught Violet's eye. It came from the sheriff's badge on Jen's coat. "The jacket!" she exclaimed. "Pressler put a bug in Dubowski's *jacket!* When Dubowski died, Pressler wanted to get the bug back before anyone could find it. He paid someone to burgle the coroner's office and take the jacket along with a few other items so no one would suspect what he was really after."

"We didn't see a jacket when we searched Pressler's house," said Jen with a frown.

Violet shrugged. "Maybe he has a secret hiding place?"

"But why wait till now to get *rid* of the jacket?" asked Cy.

"Maybe we distracted him with the whole Wade Browning thing. Now that that's over—"

"You know, I don't like being spied on."

The three of them froze, staring, bug-eyed, at the receiver.

"If you have something to say to me, come in here where I can see you." A pause, then: *"Oh, it's you. What do you want?"*

Jen reached again for the receiver controls.

"Wait a minute," came Pressler's voice again, *"were you the one who broke in here earlier and left my front door open?"*

The reply, when it came, was garbled, distorted. There was no way to make the voice out clearly. **"Yes."**

"Why on earth did you do that?"

"So the sheriff would have cause to search your house."

"Well, they didn't find anything."

"Exactly. So they have no reason to come back, do they? No surprise entrances. We can be...undisturbed."

Violet felt goosebumps rise on the back of her neck. However unrecognizable, there was something familiar about that voice. "Jen, I think you should—"

"How the hell do you record?!" Jen looked tempted to smack the receiver.

"So, you went to a lot of trouble to have a secret meeting with me. I'm intrigued," said Pressler, though he sounded bored. *"I say again, what do you want?"*

"You passed me in the street today," said the distorted voice.

"How come the other person's voice is all garbly?" asked Cy.

"You saw me, then you looked away, pretended you hadn't seen me."

"Probably 'cause they're too far away from the bug," said Jen, still fiddling with the controls.

"Are you here for an apology?" Pressler asked sardonically.

"You had a look in your eye. The same look you have now... You know, don't you."

"Know what?"

An ominous, metallic *click.*

"That I'm Veil's serial killer."

Deathly, infinite silence...

"Well, obviously," said Pressler.

With the force of a cannonball, Jen shot from her office and bolted toward her vehicle outside, already shouting instructions over her radio. Two young women were left in the office, listening to the most awful conversation they'd ever heard.

"You know," said Pressler, sounding almost amused, *"for so long, I've prided myself on being able to intuit any person's character. Between you and the Grogans, you make me see what a fool I am. You'd think I'd be crushed, but it's—hah! It's actually freeing!"* He laughed cheerily. *"When I stumbled across your little homicide last year, I thought you must have done it for some personal reason. I thought the universe had handed you to me on a silver platter—a Veil resident capable of murder, and I had just the leverage to create my very own assassin-for-hire! Of course, I thought I'd be using you to take care of someone a bit more important than Rob Mulroy, but..."*

"What?!!" gasped Cy.

"When Mulroy's body turned up the way it did, I thought you'd tried to dispose of it and gotten careless. You told me you had no idea how the serial killer got hold of it, and I swallowed your story whole. It never even occurred to me that the killer I'd hired—was the killer! Hah! Just how many victims have you claimed? I know you started at least thirty years ago, with Sheriff Grogan's childhood friend."

Cy and Violet looked at each other in shock.

"I wondered how much you'd put together," said the killer mildly.

"Enough to make sure that if anything happens to me, certain evidence will be found—"

"You mean this evidence?"

A moment of silence, and then a note of grim resignation entered Pressler's tone. *"Yes...that."*

"Hurry, Mom," Cy whispered desperately, clutching Violet's arm. "Come on, Mom, come on!"

In her head, Violet thought hard at Pressler: *Say their name, please! Say the killer's name!*

"Am I allowed a last request?" asked Pressler.

"Why not?"

"If you would just satisfy my curiosity: why are you doing this? Why kill all these people? What can you possibly get out of it?"

"I made a promise."

Violet shuddered.

"That's it? A promise? That is by far the stupidest reason I can think of. What a disappointment. You won't get away with it, incidentally."

"I already have."

"No, you haven't. I can see it in your eyes. Whatever your goal is, you're close, but you're not there yet. And I'm not the only person who can stop you."

"Who else?"

Silence...

"It's Violet, isn't it," said the killer. *"Violet and her perfect memory."*

"She's onto you," warned Pressler, *"even if she doesn't know it yet. Sooner or later she'll piece it together, as I did."*

"Well, then I'll just have to kill her, too."

Cy and Violet almost had to cover their ears, Pressler's laugh was so loud. It was the most hearty, boisterous, full-throated laugh Violet had ever heard. *"You go ahead and try!"* Pressler guffawed. *"It'll be your downfall!"*

"Why?"

"Because I know who Violet really is! Just a few minutes ago, when I came home, I got it! After all this time, I've finally found out! She is the last *person you want to cross! She's really—"*

BANG.

Cy shrieked and clung to Violet.

Something heavy slumped to the floor.

"I don't care."

Numb with horror, Violet barely felt Cy sobbing into her arm. She held the girl tightly, wishing the warmth of her friend's body would drown out what she'd just witnessed.

Less than a minute later came the sounds of banging doors, running footsteps, a woman's heavy breathing, and then Jen Grogan's grave voice…

"I'm too late."

WINTER IN VEIL

A Mystery Novella Series
by Miles Ledoux

#1 VIOLET
#2 GOOD WITCH, BAD WITCH
#3 JOHNSON'S WELDER
#4 RING AROUND THE ROSIE
#5 POP GOES THE WEASEL
#6 APRIL
#7 OVERKILL
#8 THE THIRD WILL
#9 SALT & VINEGAR
#10 MEMORY LANE
#11 THE IMPOSTOR
#12 KISS ME QUICK
#13 BEHIND THE DARKNESS

Next time in Veil...

"I want to share something about Mayor Pressler. Something I'll always remember, regardless of my history with him. Pressler and I... We weren't friends. Not at all. But just before he died, he did something for me. I was listening when it happened. The person who took his life also threatened my life. And Pressler... Pressler tried to save me by lying, by tricking the killer. He didn't have to do that. To be honest, I don't know why he did. But if he were here, I'd thank him. And I would promise him... I *promise*... I'll find whoever did this to him. And they will pay."

About the Author

Miles Ledoux was born in upstate New York and started writing murder mysteries at the age of nine. His first paid writing gig was in 2007, when a local theatre chose one of his plays for their summer melodrama. He received other royalties after moving to Los Angeles for graduate school, where he wrote, directed, and produced several mystery dessert theatre plays. He also started a side business designing and running mystery party games while working as a martial arts instructor.

Currently the author resides in Springfield, Vermont. Despite having lived in five different states, he has remained active in community theatre as a playwright, director, and actor. He also has a YouTube channel where he compares Agatha Christie adaptations to the books they were based on. His handle is @MysteryMiles.

Miles loves books, cats, music, Star Trek, Peanuts, and owns an ever-growing number of variations of the board game Clue. His favorite author is Lloyd Alexander.

You can connect with me on:

🌐 https://www.ledouxmysteries.com